REVENGE OF THE SITH ™

STAR WARS®

EPISODE III

REVENGE OF THE SITH™

Patricia C. Wrede
Based on the story and screenplay
by George Lucas

SCHOLASTIC INC.

New York   Toronto   London   Auckland   Sydney
Mexico City   New Delhi   Hong Kong   Buenos Aires

ISBN-13: 978-0-439-13929-8
ISBN-10: 0-439-13929-5

20 19 18   15 16 17 18/0

Printed in the U.S.A.
First printing, May 2005

REVENGE OF THE SITH ™

A long time ago, in a galaxy far, far away. . . .

The Republic was at war. For two thousand years, the Jedi Knights had kept the peace, but even their formidable skills could not prevent the strife this time. Led by the former Jedi, Count Dooku, the Separatist coalition broke away from the Galactic Republic. War erupted during a rescue mission on Geonosis, and many Jedi died. Jedi Master Yoda arrived unexpectedly with clone troops, in time for the Republic to win that first battle — but too late to stop the war.

At first, many in the Republic were sure that their clone troopers would end the war quickly. But the Trade Federation, with its enormous army of droids, supported the Separatists. Even with the forced-growth techniques of the clone masters, it took longer to grow a clone trooper than to produce a battle droid. The Clone Wars raged on, and spread to many systems.

Only the Jedi were not surprised. For on Geonosis, Obi-Wan Kenobi and his Padawan apprentice, Anakin Skywalker, had learned that Count Dooku had turned to the dark side of the Force — and the power of the dark side had been growing for years. The Jedi knew that defeating the Separatists would be neither quick nor easy with a Dark Lord of the Sith aiding them.

As soon as they recovered from the injuries they had received during their battle with Count Dooku, Anakin Skywalker and Obi-Wan Kenobi rejoined the war. Together they became heroes of the Republic, sometimes leading clone troopers in pitched battles, sometimes making daring raids in secret. For their work, Anakin was made a full Jedi Knight, and Obi-Wan was given a seat on the Jedi Council and the title of Master.

No one, not even the Jedi, knew that one of the things driving Anakin was his desire to be back on Coruscant, the home of the Galactic Senate. In defiance of the Jedi Order, he had secretly married Senator Padmé Amidala, who spent most of her time working there. As the fighting spread into the Outer Rim Worlds, the moments Anakin could steal to be with his wife became fewer.

Then the Separatists struck a paralyzing blow, straight at the heart of the Republic. A fleet of ships commanded by the dreaded Separatist General

Grievous slipped through the outer line of defenses to attack Coruscant itself. In the confusion the Separatists kidnapped Supreme Chancellor Palpatine, the elected leader of the Republic.

But Coruscant was not only the heart of the government and the location of the Galactic Senate. It was also the home of the Jedi Temple. As the Separatist attack began, a message was beamed to the Outer Rim, summoning the Jedi's greatest warriors home. Before the Separatist fleet could leave the Coruscant star system with the Chancellor, they found themselves under attack. Waves of clone starfighters, led by Obi-Wan and Anakin, stormed around their ships. . . .

Laser beams flashed around Obi-Wan's Jedi Interceptor as his fingers danced across the controls. The small starfighter danced in response, avoiding the beams. *Space is* supposed *to be empty,* Obi-Wan thought as he wove through the swarm of droid tri-fighters.

Not that the space around Coruscant had ever been empty. The capital planet of the Galactic Republic attracted thousands of ships every day, carrying diplomats and Senators, tourists and refugees, food and goods from strange and distant star systems. The ships that filled the sky now, however, were fighters and cruisers and battleships, not freighters and transports.

At least a lot of them are ours, Obi-Wan thought. His ship rocked as a droid fighter exploded a little too close by. Anakin had scored a hit. Obi-Wan grimaced. He didn't enjoy this sort of flying, not the way his former apprentice did. "Flying is for droids," he muttered.

As the fireball cleared, Obi-Wan saw movement against the stars. "Look out," he said into his comm. "Four droids, inbound."

He swerved as he spoke to avoid the oncoming tri-fighters. Off to one side, Anakin's Interceptor made the same move in perfect unison. They swept around one side of the droid formation, then swooped unexpectedly close to the two nearest ships. One droid saw them and followed, but the ship behind it kept to its original course, and the two fighters collided.

Two down, two to go. But the remaining droids wouldn't fall for the same trick. "We've got to split them up!" he said into the comm.

"Break left," Anakin's voice said in his ear. "Fly through the guns on that tower."

"Easy for you to say," Obi-Wan grumbled as he sent his fighter hurtling toward the gun towers of the nearest cruiser. "Why am I always the bait?"

"Don't worry," Anakin said soothingly. "I'm coming around behind you."

Obi-Wan would have snorted, but he was too busy with the controls. Flying this close to a large starship was tricky, even with the Force to help. The droids weren't having much trouble, though. Both of them had stuck with him, and they were gaining.

Laser fire flashed, barely missing the Jedi fighter.

"Anakin, they're all over me!" Obi-Wan complained.

"Dead ahead!" Anakin's voice said happily. "Move to the right so I can get a clear shot at them. Closing . . . Lock onto him, Artoo!"

Obi-Wan heard a faint beep in the background from Anakin's astrodroid, R2-D2. A moment later, one of the tri-fighters behind him exploded. Obi-Wan would have been better pleased if the second fighter hadn't kept on firing. Its aim was improving, too. That was the trouble with droids; you couldn't distract them. "I'm running out of tricks here," Obi-Wan said to Anakin.

The cruiser dropped away behind them. Out in open space, he was a sitting duck. He needed something else to dodge behind. A Separatist battleship loomed — not the best idea, perhaps, but the only one available at the moment. "I'm going down on the deck," he told Anakin. He swung his fighter, narrowly avoiding another barrage of laser fire.

"Good idea." Anakin sounded cheerful. "I need some room to maneuver."

What, space isn't big enough? But once again Obi-Wan was too busy skimming the surface of a battleship to speak. And this one was firing at him, right along with the droid fighter on his tail. *This may not have been such a good idea*, he thought as he dodged blasts coming from all directions.

"Cut right!" Anakin said, and for the first time his voice sounded a little strained. "Do you hear me? Cut right! Don't let him get a handle on you." The comm crackled, but did not cut off. "Come on, Artoo, lock on!" Anakin said. "Lock on!"

"Hurry up," Obi-Wan said. "I don't like this." A laser blast struck one of his wings. The ship bucked and twisted. Obi-Wan's hands flickered from one control to another. Behind him, his astrodroid beeped emphatically. "Don't even try to fix it, Arfour," Obi-Wan told it. "I've shut it down." So dodging the droids would be even harder. If Anakin didn't hurry . . .

As if he could hear Obi-Wan's thoughts, Anakin said, "We're locked on. We've got him," and an instant later, the droid tri-fighter exploded. "Good going, Artoo!"

Obi-Wan blew out a quiet sigh of relief. "Next time, *you're* the bait," he told Anakin. He could picture his former Padawan's answering grin, and added firmly, "Now, let's find the command ship and get on with it."

"Straight ahead," Anakin responded. "The one crawling with vulture droids."

"I see them." They were hard to miss; dozens of the broad, half-flattened shapes crouched ominously behind the blue force field that shielded the open hangar. "Oh, *this* should be easy," Obi-Wan said sarcastically.

"Come on, Master," Anakin said. "This is where the fun begins!"

Obi-Wan shook his head, though Anakin couldn't see him. They'd taken on similar odds before, and won ... barely. If this had been an ordinary battle, Obi-Wan might have joined Anakin. *Though I wouldn't have been happy about it.* But a mistake now might cost the Chancellor's life. "Not this time," Obi-Wan said. "There's too much at stake. We need help." He changed the comm's settings and called in the nearest squad of clone fighters.

A moment later, he was glad he had. The droids lifted off, rising from the hangar in a dark cloud. They headed straight for Anakin and Obi-Wan.

The clone squad of ARC-170 starfighters swung into formation behind them. Obi-Wan just had time to acknowledge their arrival before the Separatist droids were on them. He blasted one, then swung to back up Anakin. More droid fighters appeared from behind the cruiser.

Obi-Wan fired at one droid, dodged a series of laser blasts from two others, and called a warning. "Anakin, you have four on your tail!"

"I know, I know."

"And four more closing from your left."

"I know, I know!" Anakin's ship swung wildly from side to side, dodging laser fire. "I'm going to pull them through the needle."

Obi-Wan stared at the Trade Federation battle-ship. At the end of a long trench, a conning tower stood on two metal struts like legs, with only a narrow slit between them. Anakin was right; the droid fighters would never make it through that. Even a Jedi could easily crash. "Too dangerous," he warned. "First Jedi rule: Survive."

Another burst of laser fire erupted around Anakin's ship. "Sorry, no choice," Anakin said. His fighter dodged and shuddered. "Come down here and thin them out a little."

Obi-Wan shook his head again, but he plunged toward the eight vulture droids as Anakin's fighter shot down the trench toward the impossibly narrow slit ahead.

The laser fire was nearly continuous. *Where is Obi-Wan?* Anakin thought as he made his ship jump and dodge. He felt a larger explosion somewhere behind him and glanced at his rear viewscreen. Several of the vulture droids had vanished in a large fireball. *Good. Now if the rest of them will just keep following me. . . .*

The "needle" was getting close. R2-D2 beeped nervously. "Easy, Artoo," Anakin said. "We've done this before."

"Use the Force," Obi-Wan's voice said over his

comm unit. "Feel yourself through; the ship will follow."

As if I didn't know that already. It annoyed Anakin when his former Master treated him as though he were still a Padawan learner, instead of a full Jedi Knight, just as good as Obi-Wan was. *Or better.* But there wasn't time now to be annoyed with Obi-Wan, not with the conning tower almost on top of him.

R2-D2 squealed in panic as Anakin tilted the ship sideways just in time to skim through the gap. "I'm through!" he broadcast to Obi-Wan.

He pulled out, away from the battleship, and saw Obi-Wan's fighter driving the last of the vulture droids into a fireball clinging to the legs of the conning tower. *Tried to follow me and missed,* Anakin thought with satisfaction.

Obi-Wan pulled up long before he was close to the tower, and the two Jedi Interceptors flew side by side. Around them, the clone starfighters dodged and wove and fired in a deadly dance with a huge cloud of vulture droids. The clones were badly outnumbered.

"I'm going to help them out!" Anakin said, and started to turn his fighter.

"No," Obi-Wan told him firmly. "They're doing their job so we can do ours. Head for the command ship!"

Anakin complied, feeling irritated again, though

this time he was more annoyed with himself than with Obi-Wan. He *had* forgotten, just for a second, that winning the battle wasn't important — not if the command ship got away with Supreme Chancellor Palpatine.

Two droid tri-fighters appeared straight in front of them, firing missiles. Anakin called a warning to Obi-Wan as he sent his own ship sharply to the right. Two missiles pursued him. *Let's see them follow this,* Anakin thought, and went into a tight loop. The missiles collided and exploded. Anakin looked for Obi-Wan, just as Obi-Wan's voice came over his comm: "I'm hit!"

Anakin's heart lurched. Frantically, he hunted for Obi-Wan's ship. It looked intact — and then he saw the buzz droids crawling like spiders over its surface, ripping holes in the skin and tearing out wiring. At that rate, they'd destroy the fighter in a matter of minutes.

An unnatural calm descended on Anakin. "Buzz droids," he told Obi-Wan. "I see them."

There was an instant of silence as Obi-Wan absorbed the information. Then his voice came again, cool and almost resigned. "Get out of here, Anakin. There's nothing you can do."

I'll make up something. "I'm not leaving you, Master," Anakin said.

"The mission, Anakin," Obi-Wan reminded him

gently, as if he were teaching a particularly hard lesson to a reluctant Padawan. "Get to the command ship. Get the Chancellor."

Anakin hesitated. Chancellor Palpatine was not just the leader of the Republic; he was a friend and advisor. His gentle wisdom had helped Anakin many times. Only Padmé knew more about Anakin's secret feelings. But Obi-Wan had been Anakin's teacher and companion since he was nine years old. He was the father Anakin never had, the brother Anakin had imagined, the working partner who'd saved Anakin's life and been saved by him more times than either could count. Anakin set his jaw. "Not without you."

"They're shutting down the controls," Obi-Wan said.

Anakin swallowed hard. The buzz droids had already ripped Obi-Wan's astrodroid apart, so that it couldn't fix anything. Without controls, Obi-Wan would spin away into space. Even if his life support wasn't damaged, it would be hard to find him before his air ran out. And the buzz droids wouldn't stop with the controls. They'd go for the life support next.

No! Anakin came toward Obi-Wan's ship at an angle and fired. The shot vaporized several buzz droids . . . and part of Obi-Wan's left wing.

"That's not helping," Obi-Wan said.

"I agree, bad idea," Anakin admitted. *But I have to do something! What else?* "Swing right.

Steady . . ." He moved his ship closer to Obi-Wan's. Closer still . . .

"Wait!" Obi-Wan protested. "You're going to get us both killed!" He sounded as if he was more worried about what Anakin was doing than about the buzz droids.

Anakin ignored him. Obi-Wan always argued whenever Anakin wanted to try something tricky. As long as he held his ship steady, giving Anakin a stable target, he could complain all he wanted. Cautiously, Anakin dipped closer. His wing scraped away almost all of the buzz droids, but despite his care, the maneuver dented both ships — and the last remaining buzz droid ran up his wing. *Better not try that again.*

Behind him, R2-D2 beeped angrily. *Artoo can handle it,* Anakin thought. "Get him, Artoo!" he said.

"Go for the eyes," Obi-Wan advised. Anakin heard a zap, and an instant later the buzz droid slid down his wing and dropped off into space.

"Blast it!" Obi-Wan said. "My controls are gone."

He can still steer, Anakin thought. But without the rest of his controls, Obi-Wan's ship was nothing but target practice for the vulture droids. Desperately, Anakin looked for a place to hide — and saw the Trade Federation's command ship looming ahead of them.

Oh, great, just what we need . . . wait, no, it

really is *just what we need!* "Stay on my wing," he told Obi-Wan. "The general's command ship is dead ahead."

The smoke in front of Obi-Wan's fighter began to clear. A moment later, Obi-Wan's voice complained in Anakin's ears. "Whoa! Anakin, we're going to collide!"

Anakin smiled. Sometimes his Master was so predictable. "That's the plan. Head for the hangar."

The command ship loomed large in front of them. "Have you noticed the shields are up?" Obi-Wan said.

Oooops. "Sorry, Master." Anakin zipped ahead to blast the shield generator before Obi-Wan's rapidly disintegrating fighter could hit. A moment later, the two Jedi Interceptors flew through the doors of the command ship hangar. Blast doors slammed shut behind them. Obi-Wan's ship crashed at the far end of the hangar as Federation battle droids rushed in from all directions.

CHAPTER ❷

As his starfighter crashed to the hangar floor, Obi-Wan ignited his lightsaber. In one quick movement, he cut a hole in the roof of the cockpit and leaped out. Seconds later, the crippled ship exploded.

Battle droids fired as Obi-Wan landed, but he sent their laser bolts singing back at them. He sensed, more than saw, Anakin land and run to join him. Together, they cleared the battle droids from the hangar floor.

As the last battle droid fell, Obi-Wan deactivated his lightsaber and looked at his former apprentice. He knew that he ought to rebuke Anakin for taking such chances during the battle with the buzz droids. He'd risked their entire mission — and the Chancellor's life — to satisfy his personal feelings. But if Anakin hadn't taken those risks, he, Obi-Wan, would very likely be dead. Obi-Wan frowned. *He still has much to learn*, he thought, *but then, so do I.*

R2-D2 rolled forward. "Tap into the ship's computers," Anakin told the droid. R2-D2 beeped and rolled to a wall socket. Soon they had the Chancellor's location — in the sumptuous quarters at the top of the ship's spire.

Anakin frowned. "I sense Count Dooku."

That's no surprise, Obi-Wan thought. The renegade Jedi had beaten them both on Geonosis. Thanks to him, Anakin's right hand was now a mechanical skeleton instead of flesh and blood. Only the timely arrival of Master Yoda had saved their lives. Who else but Count Dooku would the Separatists send on such a crucial mission? And this time, Master Yoda was busy elsewhere. "I sense a trap."

"Next move?" Anakin asked, looking at Obi-Wan.

Obi-Wan smiled. "Spring the trap."

Anakin grinned and nodded. They left R2-D2 in the hangar and made their way through the ship. Several times, battle droids found them, but they were no match for the Jedi. Soon, they reached the elevator to the general's quarters. When the doors opened, Obi-Wan looked around carefully, but saw no sign of droids. Still, it felt wrong. And there was that other presence — "He's close," Obi-Wan told Anakin.

"The Chancellor?"

"Count Dooku."

Cautiously, the two Jedi descended the steps from the elevator into the general's quarters. The main room was enormous, but empty, except for a chair at the far end. Strapped in the chair was Supreme Chancellor Palpatine.

He doesn't look hurt, Obi-Wan thought as they walked forward. *But he's not happy. Well, who would be, under these circumstances?*

"Are you all right?" Anakin demanded as they reached the Chancellor.

"Anakin," the Chancellor said quietly, "droids." He made a small gesture with his fingers, all he could manage with the energy bonds restraining him.

As one, Obi-Wan and Anakin turned. Four super battle droids had come in behind them. Anakin smiled. "Don't worry, Chancellor. Droids are not a problem."

Don't get cocky, my young Padawan, Obi-Wan almost said, but he couldn't scold Anakin in front of the Chancellor. Especially since it would probably make Anakin even more reckless once the fight started. And there was still —

Before he could even finish the thought, Obi-Wan felt his eyes drawn upward. Tall, elegant, and graceful, Count Dooku strode onto the balcony. His face wore the same faintly amused smile Obi-Wan remembered so vividly from their last encounter.

"This time, we do it together," Obi-Wan said quietly

to Anakin. He hoped his former apprentice wasn't going to be difficult. They couldn't afford to lose.

To his surprise, Anakin gave a small nod. "I was about to say that."

Maybe he's learned more than I thought. Obi-Wan shifted his balance, waiting for the next move.

"Get help!" Palpatine said urgently from behind them. "You're no match for him. He's a Sith Lord."

And where do you think we can get help from, Chancellor? Obi-Wan gave Palpatine a reassuring smile. "Our specialty is Sith Lords, Chancellor."

As Obi-Wan and Anakin ignited their lightsabers, Count Dooku jumped down from the balcony. He landed lightly, and Obi-Wan felt the dark side of the Force surging around him. "Your swords, please, Master Jedi. Let's not make a mess of this in front of the Chancellor."

Obi-Wan and Anakin ignored him. Lightsabers ready, they closed in. As Dooku reached for his own lightsaber, they charged. Dooku met them with a mocking smile. "Don't assume that because there are two of you, you have the advantage," he said.

Count Dooku deserved his reputation as a master of the old style of lightsaber fencing. Even with both Anakin and Obi-Wan pressing him, he seemed at ease. The Jedi used every trick they knew, leaping and striking from unexpected directions. Dooku blocked them all. *At least he's not having any more luck hitting us than we are hitting him*, Obi-Wan thought. *That's a big improvement over last time.*

Anakin seemed to be thinking along the same lines. In a lull between fierce exchanges, he gave Dooku a frightening smile and said, "My powers have doubled since we last met, Count."

No, Anakin, Obi-Wan thought. *Don't taunt him.* Anger fed the dark side; they didn't need Dooku's power to be any greater than it already was.

"Good," the Count said calmly. "Twice the pride, double the fall. I have looked forward to this, Skywalker."

Despite the Count's confidence, the two Jedi forced him slowly backward. When the super droids got in the way, they cut them down. At last they reached the first set of stairs to the balcony. As the Count started up, Obi-Wan disengaged and ran to the second set of stairs to attack him from behind. Climbing the stairs, it cut down two of the super battle droids.

He can't fight in two directions at once, Obi-Wan thought as he came up behind the Count. *If we can —*

Count Dooku half-turned and raised a hand. A rush of dark power lifted Obi-Wan off his feet and choked the air from his lungs. He reached for the Force to counter Dooku, but the attack had been too sudden. He saw Dooku twist, kicking out at Anakin with all his weight behind it. Anakin fell backward, and Dooku hurled Obi-Wan over the edge of the balcony.

Obi-Wan dropped to the floor below and lay half-stunned. Distantly, he felt a surge in the dark side, and then a large chunk of the balcony hurtled down at him. His last thought before he lost consciousness was, *It's up to Anakin now.*

As the balcony collapsed atop Obi-Wan, Anakin rushed at the Count and kicked him over the edge, then followed him down. He wanted to rush to the pile of rubble burying Obi-Wan, but he knew he couldn't. *It's up to me now. I can't give Dooku even the smallest opening.* He tried to concentrate on Dooku, but his fear for Obi-Wan was hard to ignore.

Dooku smiled, and echoed Anakin's thoughts. "I sense great fear in you, Skywalker." He shook his head, as if Anakin were a particularly slow student. "You have power, you have anger — but you don't use them."

And I'm not going to, Anakin told himself. *That's the way to the dark side.* Pushing his fear aside, he tried to forget the balcony crushing Obi-Wan and the intent expression on the Chancellor's face as he watched the battle that would decide his fate. Anakin made himself focus on the fight, and only the fight.

All of the super battle droids had been cut down;

only Anakin and Dooku were left. Down the long length of the room they fought, neither one able to gain an advantage. *He's old,* Anakin thought. *Maybe I can just outlast him.* But the power of the dark side flowed around him, denying that possibility. The dark side would keep Dooku going as long as he needed. *What am I going to do? I have to beat him, or the Chancellor and Obi-Wan are dead. Not to mention me. . . .*

Behind him, he heard Chancellor Palpatine calling something, trying to be heard over the crackle and hum of the lightsabers. "Use your aggressive feelings, Anakin! Call on your rage. Focus it, or you don't stand a chance against him."

Anakin hesitated. The Chancellor was no Jedi; he couldn't know about the dangers of the dark side. He only cared about getting out of there alive. *And there's only me to do it.* Surely he could risk the dark side just this once, in order to save the Chancellor and Obi-Wan. He looked at Dooku and let himself feel the emotions that he had been keeping so tightly controlled.

Rage poured through him. This was the man who had belittled him, who had kidnapped Palpatine and nearly killed Obi-Wan, who had cut off Anakin's hand and tried to have Padmé put to death. Anakin used his anger the way he normally used the Force, letting it guide his lightsaber. Faster and faster he moved, and then his lightsaber came down and severed Count Dooku's hands.

Leaning forward, Anakin caught the Count's lightsaber as it fell. The anger still sang in his veins. He set the two lightsabers against the Count's neck and stood panting with the effort of trying to control himself.

"Good, Anakin, *good*," Palpatine said. He was smiling in relief. "I knew you could do it." Anakin felt himself begin to relax at the sound of that gentle, familiar voice. Then Palpatine said, "Kill him. Kill him now!"

Anakin stared at the Chancellor in shock. Dooku seemed just as stunned.

"Finish him, Anakin," Palpatine repeated.

Anakin swallowed hard, fighting the anger that still burned inside him. "I shouldn't — "

"Do it!" the Chancellor snapped.

Dooku tried to speak, but Anakin's hands were already moving. The lightsabers cut through the Count's neck effortlessly. Anakin stared down at the headless body, shaken. *I couldn't stop myself. I couldn't . . .* He deactivated the lightsabers, wondering what Dooku had wanted to say.

"You did well, Anakin," Palpatine said. "He was too dangerous to be kept alive."

"He was a defenseless prisoner," Anakin said bitterly. He looked at Palpatine reproachfully, and realized that the Chancellor was still strapped in the general's chair. He reached for the Force and disengaged the energy restraints. *Of course the Chancellor doesn't understand*, he told himself. Palpatine wasn't a Jedi. Furthermore, he had been trapped, and it must have seemed to him that the only way he would get free was if Anakin killed Dooku. Still, Anakin tried to explain. "I shouldn't have done that, Chancellor. It's not the Jedi way."

Palpatine stood up, rubbing his wrists. "It's only natural. He cut off your arm, and you wanted revenge. It's not the first time, Anakin."

Anakin shook his head. He knew what Palpatine meant. When the Sand People killed his mother, he had massacred them all — men, women, and children. He still dreamed, sometimes, about the children. Palpatine and Padmé were the only ones who knew about the revenge he had taken. Padmé had been horrified as much by Anakin's grief as by what he had done; Palpatine called the killings "regrettable." Neither truly understood how a Jedi would feel about it. And he *couldn't* tell another Jedi, not even Obi-Wan. Especially not Obi-Wan.

The Chancellor nodded, as if he understood what Anakin was thinking, but all he said was, "Now we must leave."

As if to underline the Chancellor's words, the floor began to tilt as the gravity generators shifted. Anakin ran to the fallen balcony that buried Obi-Wan. Using the Force, he lifted the tangled mass away, then knelt to check on his friend. *No bones broken, breathing's all right.* Anakin heaved a sigh of relief.

"There is no time!" Palpatine called urgently as he mounted the steps to the elevator. "Leave him, or we'll never make it."

"His fate will be the same as ours," Anakin said quietly. Never again would he lose someone he loved, the way he had lost his mother. Bending over, he slung Obi-Wan's unconscious body across his shoulders. He staggered under the weight, then caught his balance and headed determinedly toward the elevators.

CHAPTER 3

Slowly, Obi-Wan came back to consciousness. He felt as if he had been pounded all over — in fact, his head was still pounding. And something was digging into his stomach. Carefully, he opened his eyes. He saw a distorted Chancellor Palpatine, reaching down toward him past some sort of screen; beyond was only blackness.

Obi-Wan blinked. The Chancellor wasn't reaching down toward him; he was *below* Obi-Wan, hanging onto something. The blackness was some sort of darkened shaft. "Have I missed something?"

"Hang on," Anakin's muffled voice came from behind him. "We're in a bit of a situation."

Ah. The thing digging into his stomach was Anakin's shoulder, then, and the Chancellor was hanging on to Anakin's ankle. Obi-Wan nodded pleasantly at Palpatine. "Hello, Chancellor. Are you well?"

Palpatine glanced down at the emptiness beneath them. "I hope so."

Obi-Wan's head began to clear. "Where's Count Dooku?"

"Dead," Anakin said shortly, in the tone that meant he did not want to discuss it.

"Pity," Obi-Wan said. "Alive, he could have been a help to us."

"The ship's breaking up," Anakin snapped. "Could we discuss this later?"

Touchy, touchy. But Anakin had saved his life again, *and* he had gotten the Chancellor out unaided. He was allowed to be a little touchy. Obi-Wan stared down at the seemingly bottomless pit.

Gravity shifted, and suddenly they were hanging over a steep slope instead of a bottomless pit. Obi-Wan heard a *chunk-thump* from overhead, and looked up to see something coming toward them. The ceiling? "What's that?"

"Artoo," Anakin said. "I asked him to activate the elevator."

"Oh." So they were in an elevator shaft. Had Anakin gotten tired of waiting? *I don't think I want to know exactly how we got into this,* Obi-Wan decided. *I'll be happy if we can just get out of it.*

Anakin was shouting into the comlink, telling R2-D2 to shut down the elevator. "Too late!" Obi-Wan said. "Jump!"

They jumped. Several floors below, they hit the side of the shaft, sliding along its length ahead of the rapidly moving elevator. Gravity continued to

27

shift until the shaft was horizontal. Their speed slowed as the "slope" they were sliding down leveled off. Unfortunately, the elevator didn't pause.

"Stop the elevator, Artoo!" Anakin yelled at the comlink as they scrambled to their feet.

The elevator stopped. Then, with a horrible grinding noise, it started up again. The three men ran down the shaft, barely staying ahead of it. *The control wires must be damaged*, Obi-Wan thought.

The elevator sped up. Anakin was yelling into the comlink again, but Obi-Wan couldn't make out the words. Then Palpatine stumbled. Obi-Wan caught his arm and urged him forward. *He can't keep this up*, Obi-Wan thought. *Come on, Anakin, come up with something!*

Suddenly, all the doors in the elevator shaft flew open. Barely ahead of the rogue elevator, Obi-Wan, Anakin, and Palpatine fell through into the hallway below.

They leaned against the wall, fighting to catch their breath. *Nothing like a brisk run to clear the cobwebs out of your thinking.* Finally, Obi-Wan straightened. "Let's see if we can find something in the hangar that's still flyable. Come on."

Gravity seemed to be working normally in this part of the ship — the halls were all nice and horizontal, just the way they were supposed to be. As they ran along one, a curtain of blue light sprang up in front of them. Obi-Wan stopped short, holding out his arms to keep Palpatine from running into it. More ray shields appeared behind them and on either side, trapping them.

"How did *this* happen?" Obi-Wan grumbled. "We're smarter than this."

"Apparently not, Master," Anakin said. "This is the oldest trap in the book." Obi-Wan glared at him, and Anakin shrugged. "Well, you're the leader. I was distracted."

"Oh, so all of a sudden it's my fault?"

"You're the Master," Anakin repeated. "I'm just a hero."

Obi-Wan snorted. "I'm open to suggestions here."

Behind the two Jedi, Chancellor Palpatine cleared his throat. "Why don't we let them take us to General Grievous? Perhaps with Count Dooku's demise, we can negotiate our release."

Obi-Wan looked at Anakin, and saw a look of utter disbelief that he knew was mirrored on his own face. *General Grievous, negotiate? When it snows on Tatooine . . .*

"I say . . . patience," Anakin said after a moment.

"Patience?" Obi-Wan stared at his former apprentice. "That's the plan?"

"A couple of droids will be along in a few moments and release the ray shield," Anakin explained. "And then we'll wipe them out. Security patrols are always those skinny useless battle droids."

As if to prove Anakin's words, a pair of battle

29

droids appeared. "Hand over your weapons," one of them said in a mechanical monotone.

"See?" Anakin said smugly. "No problem."

Behind the battle droids, a large doorway opened, revealing a line of destroyer droids. Obi-Wan glanced around; there were more on the other side of the hallway. Super battle droids appeared behind the destroyers, completely surrounding the Jedi. Obi-Wan shook his head. He and Anakin *might* cut heir way past such overwhelming force, but they couldn't do it and protect the Chancellor at the same time.

At that moment, R2-D2 entered the corridor from an adjoining hallway, screeching to a halt.

"Well," Obi-Wan said to Anakin, "What's plan B?"

Anakin looked from the droids to Chancellor Palpatine and back. "I think Chancellor Palpatine's suggestion sounds pretty good to me."

This is not a good day, Obi-Wan thought as he let the droids take his lightsaber.

Beings all over the galaxy swore that the great General Grievous had no more emotion than the droids who served him. He had been born on Kalee, and even before he became a half-Kaleesh, half-droid cyborg, he had been ruthless. Now, they said, he felt nothing at all.

But those beings were wrong, Grievous thought. There was one emotion common to man and machine, the emotion he felt watching Obi-Wan Kenobi and Anakin Skywalker as they were marched onto his bridge in electrobonds. Satisfaction. If the smooth metal mask that served as his face had been capable of it, he would have smiled.

The guards had brought along the Chancellor, of course, and a little blue astrodroid. Well, he had told them to bring *all* the intruders to the bridge when they were captured, and droids took their instructions literally. The astrodroid was unimportant. It could be reprogrammed easily, once the ship was safely back in Separatist territory.

One of his bodyguards came forward with the Jedi lightsabers. Grievous took them in his metal claw, weighing them. Every Jedi made his or her own lightsaber to be a weapon and a work of art, suited to the builder alone. A close examination of the lightsaber could tell one much about the Jedi who had created it. But there would be time for that later.

Grievous turned to his prisoners, rising to his full height. He deliberately had his leg mechanics lengthened the last time his metal limbs had been overhauled, so that when he straightened up, he towered over most beings. He enjoyed looking down on them. He liked the terror in their eyes when they wondered what terrible weapons hid behind his long cloak, and the fear when they looked up and up at his expressionless metal face.

These Jedi, however, seemed unimpressed. That would change. "That wasn't much of a rescue," Grievous told them. They didn't react. Well, he had a way to get at Jedi. It never failed. He swept back his cape, revealing the lightsabers hanging in its lining. "I look forward to adding your lightsabers to my collection," he said. "Rare trophies, they are."

Obi-Wan smiled. "I think you've forgotten, Grievous. I'm the one in control here."

Had the man gone mad? He was surrounded by enemy droids, hands bound, with no one to come to his rescue. In control? Grievous stared. "So sure of yourself, Kenobi," he purred. "But it's all over for you now.

"Artoo, now!" said Skywalker, and suddenly smoke poured from the astrodroid. Startled, Grievous turned, and an invisible hand yanked one of the lightsabers away from him. The lightsaber flew toward Obi-Wan; he grabbed it behind his back and ignited it, cutting neatly through his electrobonds. A second later, he freed Anakin.

Another invisible hand tore the second lightsaber from his grasp with a screech of metal on metal. Unbelievably, the two Jedi were free, standing back-to-back and deflecting laser fire from the droids. Even the useless little astrodroid had brought down one of his super droids with some kind of cable attachment.

Grievous backed up, leaving his droid magnaguards between him and the flying laser fire. That was what bodyguards were *for*. Some of his Neimoidian bridge crew had already been hit by reflected bolts, and he wasn't about to let that happen to him. Let the droids tire the Jedi out.

One of the pilots shouted at him over the chaos. "Sir! We are falling out of orbit. All aft control cells are dead."

"Stay on course," Grievous said automatically. He stepped back another pace, calculating furiously. Without aft controls, could they still make the jump to hyperspace? No, and as fast as the repair droids fixed something, the Republic's starfighters would blow it up again. They couldn't —

The gravity grids shifted. Suddenly, the ceiling was "down." "Magnetize!" one of the pilots shouted into the intercom.

A few of the battle droids reacted in time to stick to the floor, but most of them fell to the ceiling along with the Jedi. The Jedi, Grievous noticed with dislike, seemed to take the change in stride. They'd even used the gravity shift to cut down a few more of the droids, who hadn't adjusted quickly enough.

"The ship is breaking up!" the Neimoidian pilot cried.

Just like a Neimoidian to panic, Grievous thought. *Useless beings.* But plainly, they'd run out of time. No point, now, in staying to win this fight. Let the Jedi burn up when the crippled ship crashed.

Without warning, gravity returned to normal. The Jedi dropped to the floor and ran forward. Nearly all the droids were gone; they were coming after him, now. *Too late.* Grievous turned and threw his electro-staff upward. It hit the viewport an instant later, cracking the tough, transparent material. As the Jedi closed in, Grievous jumped with all the force his mechanical legs could provide.

The weakened viewport burst, and air rushed out of the sudden breach. Grievous let himself be sucked away from the bridge along with all the pieces of droids, bits of machinery, and dead crew. He caught a glimpse of the two Jedi and the Republic's Chancellor, clinging to a control console, and then he was outside.

As he was swept away from the ship, he pointed at the hull and triggered the built-in cable in his arm. The anchor struck solidly, attaching to the hull. He let the cable pay out until the automatic blast shield snapped shut over the broken viewport, cutting off the storm of air rushing out of the ship. Then he swung himself onto the ship's hull, his clawed metal feet digging in.

It really was convenient to have a mostly droid

body, Grievous thought as he crawled along the surface of the battleship. An ordinary being would need to breathe, would be damaged by the vacuum of space, would need special equipment to cling to the ship. For Grievous, none of that was a problem.

He reached a hatch and opened it. His calculations were correct; he was in one of the escape-pod bays. He started for the pods, then hesitated. Why not make things a little harder for those annoying Jedi? He crossed to the control panel and began flipping switches, jettisoning all the escape pods, row by row.

Finally, only one pod remained. *There*, Grievous thought. *Let's see them get out of this!* He climbed into the last escape pod and blasted away from the remains of his command ship. There were Federation ships close enough to pick him up, and the clone fighters were too busy with his droids to worry about an unarmed escape pod. He had gotten away.

And with any luck, he could lay the blame for this fiasco on Count Dooku, who wouldn't be coming back to offer his own explanations. Yes, that would do nicely. Planning rapidly, the droid general steered for the nearest battleship.

CHAPTER 4

Anakin felt the ship shudder as he and Obi-Wan cut down the last of the magnaguards. Alarms sounded. "The hull is burning up!" Palpatine shouted.

Looking up at the remaining viewport, Anakin saw sparks flying off the front of the ship. He still saw the blackness of space and the stars, so they weren't in the atmosphere yet. But if the ship was that hot already. . . . He moved toward the navigator's chair to study the readouts.

"All the escape pods have been launched," Anakin said as Obi-Wan joined him. *That has to be General Grievous's work. If we'd only been a little faster, we'd have had him!*

Obi-Wan glanced at the readouts, then at the controls. "You're the hotshot pilot, Anakin," he said, keeping his tone light. "Do you know how to fly this type of cruiser?"

Obi-wan is asking *me to pilot? He must really be worried!* Not that they had any other choices. Anakin matched his tone to Obi-Wan's, acknowledging and confirming the danger. "You mean, do I know how to *land* what's left of this cruiser."

Obi-Wan nodded. Anakin took the pilot's chair — at least the layout of the bridge was more or less the same on any starship, whether Trade Federation or Republic — and looked at the screens. He was just in time to watch a large piece of the ship break away.

"Well?" Obi-Wan said as the ship bucked and shuddered.

"Under the circumstances, I'd say the ability to pilot this ship is irrelevant," Anakin told him. "Strap yourself in."

Distantly, he was aware of Obi-Wan and Palpatine following his instructions, of R2-D2 taking up a position at the auxiliary controls, but his fingers were already busy with the unfamiliar controls. *First, stop the shooting. This switch? No . . . There.* Quickly, he tapped out a message to the Republic's clone fighters: *General Kenobi and I have taken the ship. The Chancellor is safe. Stop firing.* He signed it with his name and the code that would mark it as an authentic message, and sent it off.

Dismissing the fighters outside from his mind, he set himself to fly the ship. It was a lot like trying to fly a large rock. The cruiser had no wings or landing gear. The engines had broken off with the back half of the ship. The few steering thrusters were mostly dead, and the ones that weren't dead were so damaged that anything might happen if he fired them.

And there was no time to experiment. The ship had reached the outer atmosphere, and the friction was heating up the remains of the hull. The room shook and shivered as more pieces broke away.

From the navigator's chair, Obi-Wan calmly called out information on their hull temperature, altitude, speed. Anakin's attention was focused on the controls, not Obi-Wan, but some part of him absorbed the numbers, integrated them, used them. By luck, by instinct, by feel, Anakin flew.

They were well within the atmosphere now, and still moving far too fast. Anakin opened all the hatches and extended every drag fin that still worked, trading the growing heat from the increased friction for a decrease in speed.

For a moment, it seemed to be working. Then there was an enormous jolt, and the speed readout picked up again. "We lost something," Anakin said.

"Everything from the hangar back just fell off," Obi-Wan reported. "Not to worry — we're still flying half the ship."

Anakin spared a glance for the Chancellor, who was clinging grimly to his seat. *He's an administrator; he's not used to this.* But he didn't have time to explain things to the Chancellor, not if they were going to survive this. "I'm going to shift a few degrees and see if I can slow us down," Anakin told Obi-Wan.

"We're heating up," Obi-Wan warned, and began calling out numbers.

I know, I know. Anakin played the controls, opening and closing hatches, using steering thrusters to brake, anything to slow their fall.

Obi-Wan's steady chant broke off. "Fire ships are on the left and right."

Anakin flicked a switch, and the voice of one of the fire ship pilots filled the bridge. "Follow us. We'll put out what fire we can."

Follow you? How? But there were numbers reading out on the comm; coordinates. They'd cleared a heavy-duty landing strip in the industrial section. *Strong enough to stop what's left of this bucket of bolts, and well away from the residential areas so that if we miss, we won't set fire to a lot of apartment buildings. Somebody's thinking.*

"What's our speed?" Anakin demanded, and Obi-Wan started reciting numbers again.

Through the smoking viewport, Anakin caught glimpses of the towering buildings of Coruscant streaking past below them. *Too close. We're too low, too soon.* R2-D2 beeped madly, and Anakin gestured at one of the controls. "Keep us level," he told the droid, and went back to work to slow them down.

"Steady," Obi-Wan said. "Five thousand."

"Hang on," Anakin said. "This may get a little rough. We lost our heat shields."

"Landing strip's straight ahead," Obi-Wan said a moment later.

Too low, too fast, too hot . . . too late. This isn't a landing, it's a controlled crash. And not all that controlled. Someone had been paying attention, though; the landing platform was surrounded by emergency fire speeders. *Now if we can just hit it . . .*

The ship rocked. Anakin saw a fire speeder dodge out of the way just before they plowed into the landing platform, and then the view vanished under a thick coating of fire-suppressing foam. For an instant, he was sickeningly afraid that he hadn't cut their speed enough, and they would slide off the far side of the landing platform. Then the ship shuddered to a stop.

"Come on; let's get out of here," Anakin said, unstrapping himself from the seat. Obi-Wan and the Chancellor followed his example, and soon they ducked out an escape hatch into the open air. A shuttle waited among the emergency ships to whisk them back to the Senate.

While the medical personnel aboard the shuttle looked over the shaken Chancellor, Anakin and Obi-Wan argued about the final step of the mission.

"This whole operation was your idea," Anakin

said to Obi-Wan. "You planned it. You have to be the one to take the bows this time."

"Sorry, old friend," Obi-Wan said. "You killed Count Dooku." Anakin winced, but Obi-Wan didn't notice. He went on, "You rescued the Chancellor, and you managed to land that bucket of bolts safely. You —"

"Only because of your training, Master," Anakin said earnestly. "You deserve all those speeches." *And I certainly don't want praise for the way I killed Dooku.*

"Those endless speeches." Obi-Wan shook his head. "Anakin, let's face it — you are the hero this time. It's your turn to spend a glorious day with the politicians."

The shuttle had reached the Senate landing platform. Anakin could see Master Windu and a dozen Senators waiting to welcome the Chancellor — and to assure themselves of the Chancellor's safety. There was no time for more argument.

"Then you owe me," Anakin told Obi-Wan. "And not just for saving your skin for the tenth time."

"Ninth time," Obi-Wan corrected. "That incident on Cato Neimoidia doesn't count." Anakin rolled his eyes, and Obi-Wan smiled. "See you at the briefing."

Anakin couldn't help smiling back, but his smile faded as he followed the Chancellor out the door of the shuttle. He was no hero this time, no matter what

Obi-Wan said. *A hero wouldn't have done what I did.*

Mace Windu stepped forward to greet Chancellor Palpatine. They exchanged a few stiff words, and then the attending Senators surrounded the Chancellor, congratulating him on his safe return.

Anakin watched for a moment, feeling lost. Behind him, he heard a sudden string of beeping, and then a fussy voice said sternly, "It couldn't have been that bad. Don't exaggerate."

C-3PO! If the protocol droid was there, surely Padmé had come, too. Forgetting his depression, Anakin studied the mob of Senators, searching for his wife.

He didn't see her. He took a step forward, and the Senators began moving away from the landing platform, into the Senate Office Building.

Senator Bail Organa of Alderaan saw him and left the crowd around Palpatine to join Anakin. Together, they followed the rest.

"The Senate cannot thank you enough," Bail told Anakin. "The end of Count Dooku will surely bring an end to this war and an end to the Chancellor's draconian security measures."

Anakin winced, but the Senator's words made him feel a little better. He knew it had been wrong to kill Dooku when he was helpless, but perhaps it wasn't as awful as he thought. Chancellor Palpatine seemed to think it had been necessary, and if Bail was right and Dooku's death ended the war, billions of beings would live instead of being killed in the endless battles. Surely that made a difference? *And I'll never break the Jedi Code again*, he promised himself. Just thinking that made him happier.

Bail was waiting patiently for Anakin's response. Hastily, Anakin reviewed the Senator's last comment in his mind. "The fighting is going to continue until General Grievous is spare parts," he told Bail. "The Chancellor is very clear about that."

Bail frowned and started to say something else, but Anakin was no longer listening. He sensed something, someone, nearby, following them. He sensed — "Excuse me," he said to Bail, and started for the row of giant columns that lined the hallway.

"Certainly," the Senator said to his back.

As Senator Organa hurried after Palpatine and the other Senators, Anakin slipped into the shadows behind the pillar. He was sure — yes! He turned, and Padmé slid into his arms.

Anakin forgot about Dooku, Palpatine, and everything else. Holding Padmé, kissing her, he felt complete again. Centered. Happy.

When they broke the kiss at last, Padmé echoed his thoughts. "Thank goodness you're back. I'm whole again."

Whole. "I missed you, Padmé. I've missed you so."

She shivered in the circle of his arms. "There were whispers that you'd been killed. I've been living with unbearable dread." She clung to him, as if to assure herself that he was real.

Anakin took hold of her shoulders and gave her a little shake. "I'm back. I'm *all right.*"

Padmé smiled, and he pulled her back into his arms, wanting her close. "It seems as if we've been apart for a lifetime," he went on. "And it might have been — if the Chancellor hadn't been kidnapped, I don't think they would *ever* have brought us back from the Outer Rim sieges." He started to kiss her again, but she pulled away.

"Wait," she said. "Not here."

"No, here!" Anakin said, reaching for her again. She didn't know how much he needed her right now — her calm acceptance, her love. She didn't know about Dooku. "I'm tired of this deception. I don't care if they know we're married."

"Anakin, don't say things like that," Padmé chided. "You're important to the Republic, to ending this war." She smiled reassuringly, as if she sensed his distress. "I love you more than anything," she said softly, "but I won't let you give up your life as a Jedi for me."

"I've given my life to the Jedi Order," Anakin said slowly, meaning every word. "But I'd only *give up* my life for you."

"I wouldn't like that," Padmé said thoughtfully, and grinned at him. "I wouldn't like that at all." Anakin reached for her again, but she slipped away. "Patience, my handsome Jedi. Come to me later."

She sidestepped again, but not quickly enough to avoid Anakin's Jedi reflexes. He held her close — and this time, with the pleasant shock of their meeting fading, he felt her trembling. "Are you all right?"

"I'm just excited to see you," Padmé said, but her voice was too high and she avoided his eyes.

"That's not it." Disturbed, Anakin extended his Jedi senses. "I sense more. What is it? Tell me what's going on!"

To his distress, Padmé began to cry. "You've been gone five months," she said through her tears. "It's been very hard for me. I've never felt so alone. There's —"

Anakin could stand it no longer. There was only one thing he could think of that Padmé would be so reluctant to tell him. "Is there someone else?"

To his surprise — and relief — Padmé stopped crying. "No!" she said, with an angry sincerity that was impossible to mistake. "You still don't trust me, but nothing has changed."

But there *was* a change; he could sense it even more clearly now. "It's . . . just that I've never seen you like this."

"Nothing's wrong." Padmé turned away for a

moment, then looked back at him. "Something wonderful has happened." She hesitated, and Anakin thought *Wonderful? Then why are you so frightened? Why were you crying?* And then she took a deep breath and went on. "I'm . . . Annie, I'm pregnant."

Anakin felt his mouth drop open. Of all the things it could have been, he hadn't expected *this. A baby? We're going to have a baby?*

Padmé was looking anxiously at him, waiting for his reaction. *We're going to have a baby,* Anakin thought. "That's . . . wonderful."

Padmé closed her eyes and leaned against him. "What are we going to *do?*"

A host of unwelcome thoughts poured through Anakin's mind. They could never keep *this* a secret. *You're important to the Republic, to ending this war,* Padmé had said, but when the Jedi found out he'd married Padmé, he would have to leave the Order. How could he help the Republic then? What would Obi-Wan say when he discovered how his friend and apprentice had lied to him for so long? And what would it mean for Padmé?

Firmly, Anakin set all those thoughts aside. "It's going to be all right," he told Padmé. "We're not going to worry about anything right now." He paused, and then he started to grin. *We're going to have a baby!* "This is a happy moment. The happiest moment of my life."

CHAPTER 5

As the Neimoidian shuttle came down to Utapau, Grievous studied the area through a viewport. The planet's surface was ridged and drab, dotted with huge sinkholes where the inhabitants built their cities. The shuttle descended into one of the largest and deepest of the sinkhole-cities. A landing platform, surrounded by battle droids and super battle droids, stuck out of the sinkhole wall, and the shuttle came neatly to rest on it.

As Grievous strode out of the ship, one of the droids approached. "The planet is secure, sir," it told him. "The population is under control."

Of course, they're under control, Grievous thought. *Stupid maggots.* He didn't care about the locals. He was supposed to meet the Separatist Council here.

One of his bodyguards approached. "There is a message on the special communication channel," it whispered.

All thought of the Council vanished. Grievous

hurried to the hologram area. Blue light flickered above the hologram display disc, then formed into the image of a hooded figure. Grievous bowed deeply. This was the *real* leader of the Separatists, the *real* power behind the war. "Yes, Lord Sidious," Grievous said.

"I suggest you move the Separatist Council to Mustafar," said the soft, cold voice.

"Yes, Master," Grievous replied.

"Good. The Jedi will exhaust their resources looking for you. I do not wish them to know of your whereabouts until we are ready."

That probably means it will be a long time before the fighting begins again, Grievous thought. He hid his disappointment, and instead said, "With all due respect, Master, why did you not let me kill the Chancellor when I had the chance?"

"It was not the time," Darth Sidious replied. "You must have patience. The end of the war is near, General, and I promise you, victory is assured."

Grievous nodded. But for all his power and confidence, Darth Sidious was not a fighter. *Does he understand how much that useless raid on Coruscant cost us?* A little tentatively, Grievous pressed. "But the loss of Count Dooku?"

Darth Sidious' smile was only just visible below his hood. "The death of Lord Tyranus was a necessary loss," he said. "I will soon have a new apprentice —

one far younger and more powerful than Lord Tyranus."

Somewhat reassured, Grievous nodded. But when the transmission faded, he sat studying the empty air where Darth Sidious' image had been projected. Sith Lords were tricky and treacherous. He would share more of Darth Sidious' confidence, Grievous thought, if he had a clearer understanding of Darth Sidious' plans.

Padmé woke suddenly, alone in the large bed. She lay still for a moment, gathering her thoughts. She had not slept well for months, not since she discovered her pregnancy, but this time something felt wrong. Then she realized what it was. She was *alone*.

"Anakin?"

No response. Frowning, Padmé slid out of bed to look for her husband.

She found him on the veranda, looking out at the lights of Coruscant. Tonight, the glowing strings of amber were patchy. Black, empty spaces betrayed the spots where the battle with the Separatist forces had blown up buildings. In some places, smoke from still-smoldering rubble blurred the running lights of the emergency vehicles still working to rescue beings trapped in the wreckage.

Padmé joined Anakin. He did not look at her,

even when she took his hand, but she could see light reflecting from the shine on his cheeks. He had been weeping.

"What's bothering you?" she asked, though she thought she knew.

"Nothing." Anakin's voice was low.

"Anakin," Padmé said, very gently, "how long is it going to take for us to be honest with each other?"

For a moment, she thought he would remain silent. "It was a dream," he said at last. He spoke heavily, as if saying the words made something real, something that he would prefer to disbelieve.

A dream? That was not what she had been expecting. "Bad?" she asked cautiously.

"Like the ones I used to have about my mother, just before she died."

Padmé caught her breath. Anakin had dreamed about his mother's suffering and torment for weeks. The dreams had finally driven him to go to her, against the advice and orders of the Jedi . . . and he had arrived too late. He had never forgiven himself. Sometimes Padmé thought he had never forgiven the Jedi Order, either. She looked at him. She didn't think it was the memory of his failure that was upsetting him now. "And?" she prodded.

Anakin swallowed hard. "It was about you."

Me? Padmé felt a cold chill, and her hand crept up to the necklace she always wore — the carved bit of japor that Anakin had given her "to bring you good fortune" when he was nine and she fourteen. If Anakin was having those dreams again, about her, she would need all the good fortune she could get. "Tell me."

"It was only a dream," Anakin said, and looked away.

If it was only a dream, why are you so unhappy? But saying that would only upset him more. Padmé waited.

After a moment, Anakin took a deep breath. "You die in childbirth," he said flatly.

"And the baby?" Padmé spoke automatically, almost before she thought.

"I don't know."

"It was only a dream," Padmé said, but she didn't really believe that, any more than Anakin did. His premonitions had been right too often. *Maybe I should have checked with a medical droid earlier,* she thought. But she hadn't dared, for fear the secret would get out.

Anakin moved closer and put his arms around her. "I won't let this one become real, Padmé." She leaned into him, feeling safe and reassured, but she knew it was only an illusion. Anakin had saved her from war, from assassins, from battle droids, and from monsters, but this wasn't something he could cut down with a lightsaber.

Looking up at Anakin, Padmé tried for the first time

to speak aloud all the fears she had kept bottled up inside for the past five months. "Anakin, this baby will change our lives," she said slowly. "I doubt the Queen will continue to allow me to serve in the Senate." Anakin looked stricken, and she hurried on. "And if the Council discovers that you are the father, you will be expelled from the Jedi Order."

"I know." Anakin spoke the words soberly, and she knew that he'd had some of the same thoughts. But Anakin had only been thinking for a few hours; she'd had months. Months to study every angle of the box they were trapped in.

She had accepted the fact that she would have to give up her position in the Senate. It still hurt, but there were many ways for a former Senator to continue to serve. With her experience, she was sure that she could find a position on the staff of one of the other Senators. And she would have the baby to take care of and teach. But Anakin . . .

In the past thousand years, only twenty beings had left the Jedi Order. Anakin had spoken of them once, when they were talking of Count Dooku, the latest and last of the Lost Twenty. And Anakin had always wanted to be a Jedi. He had given his life to the Order — and no matter what he said, Padmé was sure that he *would* give up his life in the service of the Jedi. He had become a hero by taking on dangerous and deadly missions, several of which had nearly killed him. What would he do, if he had to give that up? What would giving it up do to him?

Hesitantly, Padmé spoke the thought that had come to her more and more often lately. "Anakin, do you think Obi-Wan might be able to help us?"

Anakin stiffened. "Have you told him anything?"

"No," Padmé said soothingly. "But he's your mentor, your best friend — he must suspect *something*."

"He's been a father to me, but he's still on the Council. Don't tell him anything!"

Padmé sighed. "I won't, Anakin." *Not until you see for yourself that we have to do this.*

"We don't need his help," Anakin said a little too firmly, as if he were trying to convince himself as much as Padmé. "Our baby is a blessing, not a problem."

It's both, Padmé thought, but she was tired of chasing the same thoughts around and around in her head. She leaned against Anakin, letting his confidence wash over her. They didn't have to settle everything tonight. For now, it was enough to think of the joy the future would bring, instead of focusing on the problems. For now.

To be invited to visit Master Yoda in his living quarters was usually a privilege and an honor, but today it was a privilege Obi-Wan would have preferred to do without. *Meeting in secret, without the full Council . . . I don't like it.* Judging from their expressions, neither did Master Yoda or Master Windu. The dark side enveloped everything in a stifling cloud, making the future unclear. Between that and the war, fear was creeping into the Jedi sanctuary. *Fear is the path to the dark side. What is happening to us?*

And now, this latest news. Master Yoda said, "Moving to take control of the Jedi, the Chancellor is."

"All on the pretext of greater security," Obi-Wan said. In the years since the start of the war, Palpatine had gathered more and more of the Senate's powers to himself. It had only been a matter of time until he came to the Jedi Order. But anticipating something did not lessen the shock when it actually happened.

"I sense a plot to destroy the Jedi," Mace Windu put in. Yoda looked at him with mild disapproval. Master Windu was a powerful warrior, but sometimes he was too quick to see plots and threats. *And after eight hundred years of training Jedi, sometimes Yoda is too patient.* But that the Chancellor wanted to *destroy* the Jedi seemed incredible. As if he sensed Obi-Wan's reservations, Mace went on, "The dark side of the Force surrounds the Chancellor."

"As it surrounds the Separatists," Obi-Wan said thoughtfully. "There is a shifting of the Force — all of us feel it. If the Chancellor is being influenced by the dark side, then this war may be a plot by the Sith to take over the Republic."

"Speculation!" Yoda said with feeling. "On theories such as these, we cannot act." He glared at Mace and Obi-Wan impartially. "*Proof* we need, before taking this to the Council."

Yes, but how are we going to get proof? Obi-Wan thought. Then he answered his own question: "The proof will come once Grievous is gone."

Mace Windu and Yoda exchanged glances. Mace's lips tightened. Then he put into words the thing all of them had avoided saying. "If the Chancellor does not end this war with the destruction of General Grievous, he must be removed from office."

"Arrested?" Obi-Wan felt cold. They were coming perilously close to treason in even discussing such a possibility.

"To a dark place, this line of thought will take us," Yoda said, echoing his thoughts. "Great care, we must take."

Great care, indeed. But if the Chancellor continued the war, what choice would they have?

CHAPTER 6

Master Yoda sat studying Anakin Skywalker. The young Jedi did not consult him often, and it was rarer still for him to request an urgent private meeting. And this trouble, at this time — *Of great importance to us all, this must be. But why?*

"Premonitions," he said aloud. Premonitions were a rare talent for a Jedi, but not unknown. Yoda had searched the paths of the future himself on occasion. No one had done so deliberately in years, however; not since the dark side began to grow, making such foresight dangerous and unreliable. But Anakin was strong in the Force, stronger than any Jedi Yoda had known in all his hundreds of years. And he had not sought the visions, that much was clear, though he was reluctant to speak too plainly of whatever he had seen. Yoda nodded encouragingly. "These visions you have . . ."

Anakin looked down. "They are of pain, suffering," he said in a low voice. "Death."

And make you afraid, they do. But afraid of what? For whom? Cautious, he must be, or he would learn no more, and without knowledge, help he could not. "Yourself you speak of, or someone you know?"

"Someone . . ." Anakin's voice trailed off, and his hands closed into fists, as if he were trying to hold on to something.

"Close to you?" Yoda prodded after a moment.

Anakin's voice, when he spoke at last, was barely a whisper. "Yes."

"Careful you must be when sensing the future, Anakin," Yoda said. "The fear of loss is a path to the dark side." *And with the dark side grown so strong, a close and easy path it is.*

To Yoda's dismay, Anakin did not seem to hear his words. His jaw clenched, and he stared at empty air, as if he were seeing his visions as they spoke, though Yoda sensed none of the changes in the Force that would normally accompany such seeing. *Remembering, he is*, Yoda decided.

At last, Anakin spoke again. "I won't let my visions come true, Master Yoda," he said in a voice of grim determination.

Ah, young one. Strong are you with the Force, but to hold back death — that strong, no Jedi is. Out of his centuries of experience, out of his memories of the thousands of shorter-lived beings he had taught and worked with and cared for, Yoda said gently, "Rejoice for those around you who transform into the

Force. Mourn them, do not. Miss them, do not. Attachment leads to jealousy. The shadow of greed, that is."

Slowly, Anakin nodded, though Yoda sensed resistance in him still. "What must I do, Master?"

"Train yourself to let go of everything you fear to lose," Yoda told him. *A hard lesson it is, but necessary.* And it was a lesson that had to be learned again and again, Yoda thought sadly, remembering the hundreds of Jedi who had already died in the Clone Wars.

The meeting with Master Windu and Master Yoda continued to worry Obi-Wan for the next several hours. He thought about it as he reviewed the latest messages from the Senate, as he prepared for the briefing he was giving, and even as he pointed out the latest battle zones for the crowd of Jedi and answered their questions in the briefing room. But he was not thinking about the Chancellor or the Jedi Council. He was thinking about Anakin.

Master Yoda and Master Windu looked at the big picture — the way that the Chancellor, the Senate, and the Jedi dealt with one another and the different powers and authority and responsibilities that belonged to each. They considered the shifting proposals, orders, and demands like beings studying moves in a game of dejarik on a holoboard.

Anakin didn't look at the big picture. Anakin saw most things on a personal level. That hadn't been a problem while he and Obi-Wan were out battling the Trade Federation in the Outer Rim — after all, a battle droid shooting at you *was* fairly personal, whatever the reason behind it. Now that they were back on Coruscant, though, Anakin would need to consider the political implications of his actions — and everyone else's. Obi-Wan worried about Anakin's reaction to the most recent developments. *Someone* should warn him about what might be coming. Obi-Wan sighed. In this case, he was the only "someone" who could give Anakin a hint. If only Anakin would listen . . .

The door of the briefing room opened. Obi-Wan looked up from the holograms and charts he was shutting down and saw Anakin hurrying toward him. "You missed the report on the Outer Rim sieges," Obi-Wan said.

"I was held up," Anakin said. He sounded tense, and more than a little preoccupied. Then he shook his head. "I'm sorry. I have no excuse."

Obi-Wan turned to shut down the last few electronic star charts. "In short, they are going very well," he said. Perhaps he could ease into politics by starting from the briefing that Anakin had missed. "Saleucami has fallen, and Master Vos has moved his troops to Boz Pity."

Anakin frowned. "What's wrong, then?" he asked bluntly.

So much for easing into the subject. "The Senate is expected to vote *more* executive powers to the Chancellor today."

"That can only mean less deliberating and more action," Anakin said with some satisfaction. Then he saw Obi-Wan's face, and his expression became puzzled. "Is that bad? It will make it easier for us to end this war."

It's not that simple! Obi-Wan bit back the words. Anakin was no diplomat; to him, it *was* simple. "Anakin, be careful of your friend, the Chancellor."

"Be careful of what?" Anakin looked more puzzled than ever.

"He has requested your presence."

"What for?"

"He wouldn't say."

That got a frown, at last. "The Chancellor didn't inform the Jedi Council?" Anakin said. "That's unusual, isn't it?"

"*All* of this is unusual," Obi-Wan told him. "It's making me feel uneasy." At least now Anakin was paying close attention. "Relations between the Council and the Chancellor are stressed."

Anakin's frown deepened. "I know the Council has grown wary of the Chancellor's power," he said. "But aren't we all working together to save the Republic? Why all this distrust?"

Because people can do more than one thing at a

time, Obi-Wan thought. *The Chancellor can work to save the Republic and work to increase his own power, both at once. And if we don't pay attention, he'll have too much power by the time the war is over.* But that would be dangerous to say aloud, even in the Jedi Temple. "The Force grows dark, Anakin," Obi-Wan said instead. "We are all affected by it. Be wary of your feelings."

Anakin nodded, but as they left the conference room together, Obi-Wan could only hope that he had said enough.

The office of the Supreme Chancellor of the Senate boasted one of the best views of Coruscant on the planet. Most windows opened only onto the shadowy gray canyons between the enormous buildings that blanketed the planet's surface. The huge skyscrapers were like manufacutred mountains, making it impossible to see very far.

But the Chancellor's office was above most of the other buildings. From its windows, the skyscrapers looked less like mountains than like a forest of petrified evergreens. Today, though, a smoky brown haze hung over the forest. Gaps in the rows of spikes marked places where buildings had been destroyed in the battle. *The Separatists have a lot to answer for*, Anakin thought.

Chancellor Palpatine broke the silence at last. "Anakin, this afternoon the Senate is going to call on me to take direct control of the Jedi Council."

Anakin's eyes widened. Obi-Wan had said that the Chancellor would be given new powers, but Anakin hadn't expected anything like *this*. "The Jedi will no longer report to the Senate?" he asked, not entirely believing it.

"They will report to me, personally," Palpatine said. "The Senate is too unfocused to conduct a war."

"I agree," Anakin said quickly. Remembering Obi-Wan's words, he added, "But the Jedi Council may not see it that way. With all due respect, sir, the Council is in no mood for more constitutional amendments."

"In this case, I have no choice," Palpatine said almost sadly. "This war must be won."

"Everyone will agree on that," Anakin said. *Though sometimes I think the Jedi Council is so worried about politics that they've forgotten what the real problem is.* As soon as he thought it, Anakin felt guilty. The Council had sent its own members into battle — and lost some of them, too. *It's being back on Coruscant instead of out in the field; it makes me feel hemmed in,* Anakin thought. *And . . . and other things.* He didn't want to think about the dreams right now.

Palpatine had been talking; Anakin brought his

attention back to the conversation in time to hear the Chancellor ask, "Don't you wonder why you've been kept off the Council?"

"My time will come," Anakin said automatically. "When I am older, and, I suppose, wiser." *But my time won't come*, he thought. *Not anymore. As soon as they find out about Padmé and the baby, I'm going to have to leave the Jedi.* Suddenly he felt empty, the way he'd felt when he was nine and the Jedi Council had said he was too old for training. *What will happen to me now?* he had asked Master Qui-Gon Jinn. He had become Qui-Gon's ward, but that hadn't seemed enough, even when he was nine. The Council had relented after Qui-Gon's death, but they'd never countenance this.

"I hope you trust me, Anakin," the Chancellor said.

"Of course," Anakin replied, feeling guilty. He didn't trust the Chancellor enough to tell him about Padmé, or the baby. But he didn't trust *anyone* enough to tell them that. Not yet.

"I need your help, son, " Palpatine said.

Did I miss something? "What do you mean?"

"I fear the Jedi. The Council keeps pushing for more control. They're shrouded in secrecy and obsessed with maintaining their autonomy — ideals I find simply incomprehensible in a democracy."

Anakin barely kept from rolling his eyes in

exasperation. Obi-Wan had said almost the same things about the Chancellor. Why couldn't they all just *stop*, and get on with fighting the war? "I can assure you that the Jedi are dedicated to the values of the Republic, sir," he said to Palpatine.

"Their actions will speak more loudly than their words," Palpatine replied. "I'm depending on you."

"For what?" Anakin asked, puzzled. "I don't understand."

"To be the eyes, ears, and voice of the Republic," Palpatine told him.

What does that *mean?* The Chancellor was the voice of the Senate, and the Senate was the voice of the Republic. Did Palpatine need a Jedi assistant? That didn't make any sense.

"Anakin," Palpatine said after a moment, "I'm appointing you to be my personal representative on the Jedi Council."

Well, *that* was clear enough. Then the words sank in. "Me? A Master?" *The youngest member of the Jedi Council ever! And maybe then they'll let me stay, even if they find out —* He wouldn't finish that thought; the hope was too great and too fragile. Besides . . . "I am overwhelmed, sir, but the Council elects its own members. They will never accept this."

"I think they will," the Chancellor said with a quiet firmness that was utterly convincing. "They need you more than you know."

CHAPTER 7

It took all of Anakin's self-control to keep from pacing up and down the hallway outside the Jedi Council chamber. His head was whirling. It had only been a few hours since Chancellor Palpatine had told him he wanted Anakin on the Jedi Council; it seemed like minutes since the Senate had given the Chancellor the powers that made Anakin's appointment official. So why did it feel as if he'd been standing out here for days?

The door opened at last, and Anakin went in. The Council chamber seemed larger than Anakin remembered. He had been there many times since the beginning of the Clone Wars, to report on the missions he and Obi-Wan had conducted, but he didn't remember it ever taking so long to cross to the center of the circle. The waiting Masters sat, expressionless, in their places — Mace Windu, Eeth Koth, Yoda, the holograms of Plo Koon and Ki-Adi-Mundi. Even

Master Obi-Wan's face gave no hint of the Council's decision.

Finally, he reached the center of the floor, stopped, and bowed to the Council.

Mace Windu spoke at last, formally, as head of the Jedi Council. "Anakin Skywalker, we have approved your appointment to the Council as the Chancellor's personal representative."

"I will do my best to uphold the principles of the Jedi Order," Anakin said with equal formality, but it was hard to contain his joy. He wanted to jump around and shout, or at least grin.

Master Yoda must have sensed some of Anakin's feelings, for he gave him a stern look. "Allow this appointment lightly, the Council does not. Disturbing is this move by Chancellor Palpatine."

"I understand," Anakin said.

"You are on this Council," Mace went on, "but we do not grant you the rank of Master."

What?! Anger swept over Anakin, and with it all his formal control abandoned him. "How can you do this? I'm more powerful than any of you! How can I be on the Council and not be a Master?"

"Take your seat, young Skywalker," Mace said, biting off the words with icy disapproval.

Anakin swallowed hard. Inside, he was still seething, but he forced out the words, "Forgive me, Master," and went to one of the empty chairs. *The*

Chancellor is depending on me; they'll never trust either of us if they think I can't control myself. But nobody has ever been on the Council who wasn't a Master! And I'm good enough. Everybody knows it.

Ki-Adi-Mundi cleared his throat, and the meeting got down to business. "We have surveyed all systems in the Republic, and have found no sign of General Grievous."

"Hiding in the Outer Rim, he is," Yoda suggested. "The outlying systems, you must sweep."

"It may take some time," Obi-Wan said. "We do not have many ships to spare."

"We cannot take ships from the front line," Mace said.

Despite his anger, Anakin found himself nodding in agreement. The Republic was spread too thinly already.

"And yet, it would be fatal for us to allow the droid armies to regroup," Obi-Wan said.

Anakin agreed with that, too.

"Master Kenobi, our spies contact, you must," Yoda said. "Then wait."

Anakin frowned. *Wait? That will give General Grievous time to regroup. But if we don't have enough fighters to send right away, what else can we do?*

The blue hologram of Ki-Adi-Mundi raised a hand. "What of the droid landing on Kashyyyk?"

Everyone agreed that they couldn't afford to lose Kashyyyk, the planet of the Wookiees. It was on the main navigation route for the whole southwestern quadrant. Anakin volunteered to lead an attack group at once; he knew that system well, so he figured it wouldn't take long. But Mace Windu shook his head. "Your assignment is here with the Chancellor," Mace told him.

Anakin swallowed his disappointment. He hadn't realized that being the Chancellor's representative would keep him away from the front lines. *They won't let me do the job I'm good at,* he thought, *and they won't make me a Master so I can be good at this job. It isn't fair!*

It didn't help to hear Yoda say, "Good relations with the Wookiees I have. Go, I will." Or to hear Mace Windu's instant agreement. All through the rest of the meeting, while the Council gave out assignments and planned the strategy of the war, Anakin's anger simmered. He held on to his temper until the Council was over. But when he and Obi-Wan started down the hall toward the briefing rooms, he couldn't resist venting his feelings.

"What kind of nonsense is this?" he grumbled. "Put me on the Council and not make me a Master? That's never been done in the history of the Jedi! It's insulting."

"Calm down," Obi-Wan said. "You've been given

a great honor. To be on the Council at your age has never happened before."

Anakin snorted. *There's never been a Jedi as strong as I am, either.*

"Listen to me, Anakin," Obi-Wan said, and the seriousness of his tone caught Anakin's attention. "The fact is, you're too close to the Chancellor, and the Council doesn't like him interfering in Jedi affairs."

Too close to the Chancellor? Does he think — "I swear to you, I didn't ask to be put on the Council," Anakin said. If that was what the other Jedi thought, no wonder they were making difficulties!

"But it's what you wanted," Obi-Wan said. "And regardless of how it happened, you find yourself in a delicate situation."

"You mean divided loyalties." *But we're all on the same side. Aren't we?*

Obi-Wan shook his head. "I *warned* you that there was tension between the Council and the Chancellor. I was very clear. Why didn't you *listen?* You walked right into it."

That was Obi-Wan, always looking for obscure motives and hidden meanings. But this time, Anakin thought, he was missing what was right in front of him. "The Council is upset because I'm the youngest ever to serve," Anakin told him.

"No, it is not," Obi-Wan said in exasperation. He

hesitated, then said more quietly, "Anakin, I worry when you speak of jealousy and pride. Those are not Jedi thoughts. They're dangerous, dark thoughts."

"Master, you of all people should have confidence in my abilities," Anakin said. Obi-Wan gave a small nod. Reassured, Anakin went on, "I know where my loyalties lie."

Obi-Wan looked at Anakin, then turned away. "I hope so."

Disturbed, Anakin waited for his former mentor to continue. When Obi-Wan said nothing, Anakin decided to push. "I sense there's more to this talk than you're saying."

"Anakin, the only reason the Council has approved your appointment is because the Chancellor trusts you," Obi-Wan said, and stopped again.

"And?" Anakin was getting tired of all these hints. *Just for once, can't you just come right out and say whatever it is?*

"Anakin, look, I'm on your side," Obi-Wan said unhappily. "I didn't want to see you put in this situation."

"*What* situation?" He couldn't mean the appointment to the Council! Obi-Wan was his friend. He knew how much Anakin wanted a seat on the Council.

Obi-Wan stopped walking and turned to face Anakin. He hesitated, as if he was searching for the right words. Then he took a deep breath. "The Council wants you to report on all of the Chancellor's dealings. They want to know what he's up to."

Anakin stared at Obi-Wan, stunned. A tiny part of his mind whispered, *Don't ever ask Obi-Wan to come right out and say something, ever again,* but most of him was trying to absorb what Obi-Wan had just said. "They want me to spy on the Chancellor?"

Obi-Wan nodded.

"That's treason!"

"We are at war, Anakin," Obi-Wan said sadly. "And the Jedi Council is sworn to uphold the principles of the Republic, even if the Chancellor does not."

Something is very wrong here. "Why didn't the Council give me this assignment when we were in session?" Anakin demanded.

Obi-Wan looked even more unhappy than before. "This is not an assignment for the record. The Council asked me to approach you on this personally."

They knew. They knew they shouldn't be asking this. Anakin's head was spinning. "The Chancellor is not a bad man, Obi-Wan," he said desperately. "He befriended me. He's watched out for me ever since I arrived here." Surely, Obi-Wan would understand. *We're on the same side! Why can't anyone else see that? We should be spying on . . . on General Grievous and the Separatists, not on a good man who's working for the same things we are!*

But Obi-Wan was shaking his head. "That is why you must help us, Anakin." But he couldn't face Anakin as he continued, "We owe our allegiance to the Senate, not to its leader . . . who has managed to stay in office long after his term expired."

Anakin stared in disbelief. *They can't blame the Chancellor for that!* "Master, the Senate *demanded* that he stay longer."

"Use your feelings, Anakin," Obi-Wan urged. "Something is out of place here."

"You're asking me to do something against the Jedi Code," Anakin pointed out bitterly. "Against the Republic. Against a mentor . . . and a friend. *That's* what's out of place here. Why are you asking this of me?"

"The Council is asking you," Obi-Wan said.

Anakin stared at his friend, feeling ill. *I promised myself, I promised, just yesterday, that I would never break the Jedi Code again.* And now the Jedi Council itself was telling him that the Code wasn't important if it got in the way of what they wanted. *Obi-Wan was asking him to do this.* "I know where my loyalties lie," Anakin repeated, feeling the hollowness of the words that, only moments ago, he had meant with all his heart.

Obi-Wan took that as an answer, and nodded in evident relief. But as he followed his former Master down the long hall, Anakin wondered how much of an answer it really was.

CHAPTER 8

The sun was setting when Padmé finally returned from the Senate. Outwardly, the entire Senate supported Chancellor Palpatine without reservation, but there was enormous tension below the surface. Most of her days now were spent discussing whether something should be done about the Chancellor, and if so, what that something should be. Padmé herself had grown more and more uneasy with Palpatine's steadily increasing power.

She had worked with Palpatine and trusted him for years, ever since her term as the elected Queen of Naboo, when he had been Naboo's representative in the Senate. She herself had challenged former Senate Chancellor Valorum, opening the way for Palpatine to take control. *Would I have done the same things*, she wondered, *if I had known what Palpatine was going to do with that control, once he had it?*

She didn't know the answer to that; but she *was* sure

that she had to do something about what was happening now. She was aware that the talks bordered on treason. After all, Chancellor Palpatine had done nothing illegal. Padmé often found herself wondering what her Jedi friends would think if they knew what she was doing. Most of all, she wondered what Anakin would think.

The airspeeder pulled up at the landing platform, and Padmé gave herself a shake. *Enough work for one day.* Her back ached and her feet hurt; the robes that hid her pregnancy were heavy and hot; and she was almost too tired to think. She had earned a rest. And she couldn't help hoping that Anakin would slip away from the Jedi Temple again. He couldn't come every night, she knew that, but he'd been away so *long*. . . .

She dismissed Captain Typho and her two handmaidens almost as soon as she was out of the speeder. "I'll be up in a while," she told them. C-3PO hovered uncertainly as they left, until she sent him to check the security droids.

When she was alone at last, Padmé sighed in relief and went out to the veranda to watch the sunset. She leaned against the railing, glad that for once she didn't have to think about what to say and whether it would provoke some thin-skinned fellow Senator.

She wasn't sure how long she'd been standing

there when she sensed someone else on the veranda. Uneasy, she turned and found Anakin standing close behind her. "You startled me!" she complained, even as she held out her arms for a quick hug.

"How are you feeling?" Anakin asked when they broke apart at last.

Padmé laughed. "He keeps kicking."

"He?" Anakin's eyes widened. "Why do you think it's a boy?"

"My motherly intuition," Padmé teased. Even if she'd consulted a medical droid, she wouldn't have asked. Wondering whether she carried a boy or a girl had been one of the few, secret pleasures she had during the long months Anakin had been away. She took her husband's hand and set it against her stomach, so that he could feel the tiny, unseen foot beating against the walls that enclosed its owner.

Anakin's eyes widened. "Whoa!" He looked at her and grinned. "With a kick that strong, it's got to be a girl."

She laughed, acknowledging the way he'd turned her teasing back on her, and he laughed with her. *This is how it should be, always*, she thought, leaning into his arms. And there was more good news to share, that would prolong the happy moment. "I heard about your appointment, Anakin," she said. "I'm so proud of you."

To her surprise, his expression darkened. "I may

be on the Council," he said angrily, "but they refused to accept me as a Jedi Master."

The fragile moment of happiness evaporated. "Patience," she told him. "In time, they will recognize your skills."

"They still treat me as if I were a Padawan learner," Anakin said, as if he hadn't heard her. He clenched his fists. "They fear my power; that's the problem."

"Anakin!" She didn't like it when he got this way, angry and resentful and eager to place the blame on someone else. *But there isn't always someone to blame — it can just be the way things are. You have to deal with it and move on.*

"Sometimes, I wonder what's happening to the Jedi Order," Anakin went on, and now he sounded sad, almost hurt, instead of angry. "I think this war is destroying the principles of the Republic."

Anakin? Padmé stared at him. In the years she had known him, she had never once heard him speak like this. Usually, Anakin refused to talk about anything remotely political. It was the one thing they had never agreed on. But now, at last, he seemed to be looking beyond the straightforward questions of which assignment he would be given and how best to complete it. It gave her the courage to say something she had been thinking for months while she watched Chancellor Palpatine grow ever stronger and more powerful: "Have you ever considered that we may be on the wrong side?"

Anakin stiffened and looked at her suspiciously. "What do you mean?"

"What if the democracy we thought we were serving no longer exists?" Padmé said, voicing her most secret fear. "What if the Republic has become the very evil we have been fighting to destroy?"

"I don't believe that, Padmé," Anakin said, a little too vehemently. "You sound like a Separatist!"

"Anakin, this war represents a failure to listen," Padmé persisted. "You're closer to the Chancellor than anyone. Please, please — ask him to stop the fighting and let diplomacy resume."

She reached out to him as she spoke, but he pulled back. "Don't ask me to do that, Padmé," he said furiously. "Make a motion in the Senate, where that kind of request belongs!" He turned away. "I'm not your errand boy. I'm not anyone's errand boy!"

Something's wrong. Padmé set her own worries aside, and gently touched his arm. "What is it?"

"Nothing." But there were worlds of anger and hurt in his tone.

She waited, hoping he would relent and explain, but he stayed stubbornly silent. "Don't do this," Padmé said. "Don't shut me out. Let me help you."

"You can't help me," Anakin told her sadly. He

tried to smile. "I'm trying to help *you*. I sense there are things you are not telling me."

Has he heard something about the talk in the Senate? Padmé stared at him. *I can't ask. If he hasn't, I'd betray people who trust me. And it isn't fair to ask Anakin to keep the secret if he doesn't fully agree with our position.* "I sense there are things *you* are not telling *me*," she said, hoping that he would open up to her at last.

Anakin's eyes widened, and he looked away. *I was right; there is something.* But he didn't say anything. *Perhaps he can't. Perhaps he's been sworn to secrecy, the same way I've been.*

She shook her head, trying to banish an image of the two of them standing close together, longing for each other but unable to pass through the invisible wall that separated them. "Hold me," she said. She reached for Anakin, trying to deny the wall, or at least make some breach in it that would bring back the hope and happiness she had felt only moments earlier. "Hold me like you did by the lake on Naboo, so long ago, when there was nothing but our love. No politics, no plotting —"

Anakin's face twisted, as if he, too, would like to recapture that magical, lost time. *Not lost, please, not lost forever.* As he took her in his arms, she finished in a whisper, "— no war," and his grip tightened. But in spite of his warm presence, she could not help feeling that they were farther apart than they had been a few days before, when he was in the Outer Rim and she was here on Coruscant.

I don't like all these good-byes, Obi-Wan thought, looking across the Jedi gunship at Mace Windu and Master Yoda. He wondered where the thought had come from. Jedi were always departing on missions; it never used to bother him, whether he was the one leaving or the one staying behind. *It's the war,* he decided. *Too many Jedi are leaving and not coming back.*

"Anakin did not take to his assignment with much enthusiasm," Obi-Wan said, breaking the silence.

"Too much under the sway of the Chancellor, he is," Yoda said, shaking his head.

"This is a dangerous move, putting them together," Mace warned. "I'm not sure the boy can handle it."

"He'll be all right," Obi-Wan said, trying to feel as confident as he sounded. "I trust him with my life."

"I don't," Mace replied.

Startled, Obi-Wan looked at Mace. Surely there was no longer any question of *trusting* Anakin! He might not be the perfect ideal of a Jedi Knight, but he had proven his abilities again and again. And besides — "With all due respect, Master, is he not the Chosen One? The One who will destroy the Sith and bring balance to the Force?"

"So the prophecy says." Mace's tone was skeptical.

"A prophecy misread that could have been," Yoda pointed out.

"Anakin will not let me down," Obi-Wan insisted. "He never has."

"I hope that right you are," Yoda said heavily as the gunship landed. The doors swung open, and the little Jedi Master rose. "And now, destroy the droid armies on Kashyyyk, I will. May the Force be with you."

Mace and Obi-Wan echoed the formal farewell as Yoda stumped down the ramp to meet the clone assault troops preparing for departure. As the gunship rose and headed for the Jedi Temple, Obi-Wan frowned. Never before had he heard the other Jedi Masters state their opinion of Anakin so plainly. And he couldn't keep from wondering . . .

How can Anakin trust us, if we don't trust him?

CHAPTER 9

Even in the middle of a war, elegance and ease filled the Galaxies opera house. The most important and cultured members of the government went there to watch the best performers in the Republic. For a few hours, they could pretend there was no war.

But even here, Anakin thought, the war had changed things. Fewer of the Senators and administrators came to the opera house; the seats were crowded with less important, less busy beings. Red-robed guards stood outside the Chancellor's private box, observing the hallway instead of the performance. The infamous Baron Papanoida loitered nearby. *I wonder what he's doing here?* But no one else looked twice at Anakin, though his plain Jedi robes made him feel a little out of place amid all the magnificence.

The guards let him into the Chancellor's box. Anakin stood for a moment, letting his eyes adjust to the dimmer light. Chancellor Palpatine was seated near the front, where he had the best view of the stage; Mas Amedda and Sly Moore sat behind him. As Anakin saw him, Palpatine raised a hand and gestured him over.

"I have good news," Palpatine said softly, as Anakin bent to hear him. "Our Clone Intelligence Units have discovered the location of General Grievous. He is hiding in the Utapau System."

"At last!" Anakin said. Mas Amedda frowned at him; feeling sheepish, he lowered his voice and went on, "He won't escape us this time."

Palpatine smiled and nodded, but Anakin wasn't sure whether the gesture was meant for him or for the Mon Calamari dancers in the liquid globe before him. "You are the best choice for this assignment," Palpatine said after a moment. "But the Council can't always be trusted to do the right thing."

"They try," Anakin said. Then he remembered the request Obi-Wan had made. *Do they?* he wondered.

"Sit down," Palpatine said. He dismissed Amedda and Sly Moore, then leaned toward Anakin. "You know I'm not able to rely on the Jedi Council. If they haven't included you in their plot, they soon will."

Anakin hesitated. "I'm not sure I understand." Spying on the Chancellor was wrong, but it wasn't a *plot*, he told himself. The Council just wanted more information.

"The Jedi Council wants control of the Republic," Palpatine said flatly. "They're planning to betray me."

No. But Anakin wasn't as certain as he'd been a few days ago. "I don't think —"

"Anakin, search your feelings," Palpatine said gently. "You do know, don't you?"

"I know they don't trust you." Even saying that much felt like a betrayal. But surely Palpatine knew it already.

Palpatine smiled sadly. "Or the Senate, or the Republic. Or democracy, for that matter."

"I have to admit, my trust in them has been shaken," Anakin said.

"How?"

Anakin couldn't think of a thing to say. He couldn't lie to the Chancellor, but telling him the truth would only make matters worse. *We're on the same side! We should be working together.*

But Palpatine nodded, as if Anakin had spoken aloud. "They asked you to spy on me, didn't they?" he asked.

He knows! Anakin looked down. "I don't know what to say." He couldn't quite bring himself to confirm the Chancellor's suspicions. "I'm confused."

"Remember back to your early teachings, Anakin," the Chancellor said. "'All those who gain power are afraid to lose it.'" He paused. "Even the Jedi."

"The Jedi use their power for good!" *The way I*

did, when I killed Count Dooku? Anakin shook off the thought. *I didn't intend to kill him. It just . . . happened. I knew it was wrong. I knew it was not the way a Jedi is supposed to use his power.* But a small voice in the back of his head whispered, *Still, you killed him.*

"Good is a point of view, Anakin. And the Jedi point of view is not the only valid one." Palpatine settled back more comfortably in his chair. "The Dark Lords of the Sith believe in security and justice also, yet they are considered —"

"— evil." Anakin was glad Palpatine had finally picked something he was sure of.

Palpatine smiled. "Evil . . . from a Jedi's point of view. Yet the Sith and the Jedi are similar in almost every way, including their quest for greater power. The difference between the two is the Sith are not afraid of the dark side of the Force. That is why they are more powerful."

"The Sith rely on their passion for their strength," Anakin said. "They think inward, only about themselves."

"And the Jedi don't?" Palpatine said, lifting his eyebrows skeptically.

"The Jedi are selfless. They only care about others."

Palpatine's smile grew. "Or so you've been trained to believe. Why is it, then, that they have asked you to do something you feel is wrong?"

"I'm not sure it's wrong." The Council must have

reasons he didn't know about for asking him to spy on the Chancellor. *But they wouldn't tell me what they were.* A cold, hard feeling grew inside him. *What if we really* aren't *all on the same side?*

"Have they asked you to betray the Jedi Code?" Palpatine asked. "The Constitution? A friendship? Your own values?"

Anakin swallowed hard and said nothing.

"Think," Palpatine urged him. "Consider their motives. Keep your mind clear of assumptions. The fear of losing power is a weakness of *both* the Jedi and the Sith."

Anakin hardly heard him. He was a Jedi; it was the only thing he'd ever wanted to be, the only dream he'd ever had. *I wanted to be the best Jedi ever!* He'd had trouble, sometimes, living up to the Code. *Like killing Dooku.* He'd always thought it was harder for him than for other Jedi because he'd started the training late, but what if that wasn't it at all? What if *nobody* else was really following the Code? He found himself wishing, with a strength that surprised him, for one of Obi-Wan's stern lectures on the importance of the Code. *I'll talk to Obi-Wan about this later,* he decided. Perhaps Obi-Wan could make sense of all this. Somehow.

The Chancellor had turned back to watch the performance. After another moment, he asked, "Have you heard the legend of Darth Plagueis the Wise?"

"No." The change of subject was a relief. Anakin

didn't want to talk about the Jedi anymore. His feelings were too confused.

"I thought not," Palpatine said. He leaned back, studying Anakin in the dim light. "It's not a story the Jedi would tell you. It's a Sith legend. Darth Plagueis was a Dark Lord of the Sith. He had such a knowledge of the dark side that he could even keep the ones he cared about from dying."

Padmé! Instantly, Anakin forgot about the Jedi Council, about spying, about Obi-Wan and the Code. "He could actually keep someone safe from death?" he asked.

"The dark side is the pathway to many abilities that some consider unnatural," Palpatine answered in a soft voice.

Remembering where they were, Anakin lowered his voice. "What happened to him?"

"Unfortunately, he taught his apprentice everything he knew — and then the apprentice killed him in his sleep." Palpatine smiled slightly. "It's ironic that he could save others from death, but not himself."

Anakin remembered bending over his dying mother, *knowing* that there was some way to save her but unable to sense what it was. *I knew the Force could keep someone from dying! I knew it! If I can find out what this Darth Plagueis learned, I can save Padmé.* Trying to keep the eagerness from his voice, he asked, "Is it possible to learn this power?"

"Not from a Jedi," Palpatine said with finality.

The ballet was ending. Palpatine joined briefly in the applause, then gestured to Anakin to precede him out the door. Anakin nodded, but he was still preoccupied with what Palpatine had told him. The Jedi archives contained considerable information about the Sith, Anakin knew, but access to that information was restricted to Jedi Masters. *And I'm not a Master.* His lips tightened in a combination of anger and determination. *I don't care. Somehow, I am going to find out how to do what Darth Plagueis did. I am going to save Padmé. I will do anything to save her.*

Anything.

Yoda's long ears drooped as he watched the hologram of Mace Windu. The senior Jedi's arguments were unchanged — if the Chancellor did not end the war once General Grievous was destroyed, he must be arrested. That was as close to proof of the Chancellor's intentions as they would ever come.

"Troubled by this, I am," Yoda told the image.

"Master Yoda, I need your vote." Mace's voice was exasperated. "We cannot wait any longer. The Chancellor is already suspicious."

Yoda scowled. "Several Jedi you will need to execute the arrest."

"I have chosen three of our best, Master." Mace

sounded as if he was trying to be patient. Yoda suppressed a snort. Master Windu was not known for his patience.

"Cunning, Palpatine is," Yoda warned. "Caught by surprise, he will not be."

"Then you support my plan?"

Yoda hesitated. *Listen, he does not. Yet move we must, or too late it will be.* "My vote you have. May the Force be with you."

"Thank you, Master."

As the hologram faded, Yoda heard a commotion behind him. He turned to find two Wookiees confronting one of the clone commanders. "Let him pass, Chewie," Yoda said.

The clone commander entered and saluted. "The clones are in position," he informed them.

Time it is to think of the present. Yoda nodded and stumped out onto the balcony where he and the commander could observe and direct the coming battle. Long practice let him focus on the needs of now, but the problem of the Chancellor lay like a bruise at the back of his mind. What would happen when General Grievous was found and defeated at last?

CHAPTER 10

*A*nakin is having trouble adjusting to his new position, Obi-Wan thought as the two men walked toward the docking bay. His former apprentice had brought the Chancellor's news straight to the Jedi Council — General Grievous was on Utapau. But Anakin hadn't been happy when the Council assigned Obi-Wan to lead the attack alone. *He needs time, that's all. Joining the Council is a big adjustment.*

It didn't help that Chancellor Palpatine had recommended Anakin for the job. *Doesn't the Chancellor realize how awkward it is for Anakin to come into the Council and say, "The Chancellor wants me to lead the attack?" It makes him sound arrogant, when he's just passing on Palpatine's requests.* But the Chancellor wasn't likely to listen to Obi-Wan's advice on how to handle Anakin Skywalker.

As they came out onto the platform above the docking bay, Anakin broke the silence at last. "You're going to need me on this one, Master," he said.

"I agree," Obi-Wan replied. When they'd rescued the Chancellor, Grievous had been too fast for both of them together; how would Obi-Wan beat the droid general alone? He forced a smile. "It may be nothing more than a wild bantha chase," he said, as much to reassure himself as Anakin.

Anakin started to say something, then stopped. Obi-Wan waited a moment. When Anakin remained silent, he turned to leave. The thousands of clone troopers didn't really need his supervision to load themselves into the transports, but it never hurt to be sure.

"Master!"

Obi-Wan stopped and looked back. Anakin walked toward him and bent his head in apology.

"Master," Anakin said again, "I've disappointed you. I have been arrogant. I have not been very appreciative of your training. I apologize. I'm just so frustrated with the Council. But your friendship means everything to me."

All Obi-Wan's love for this difficult, talented, head-strong apprentice rushed forward. Anakin had his faults, but he was a good man. He always came through. Smiling, Obi-Wan put a hand on Anakin's shoulder. "You are wise and strong, Anakin. I am very proud of you." A little embarrassed by the depth of his own feelings, he tried for a more light-hearted note. "This is the first time we've worked separately. Hopefully, it will be the last."

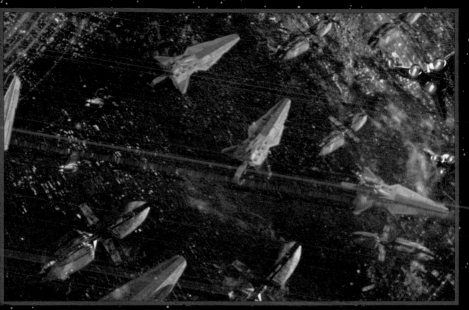

A desperate mission to rescue the captive Chancellor.

R2-D2 aids Anakin on his mission.

**Buzz droids almost destroy
Obi-Wan's Jedi Interceptor.**

Anakin cuts a hole in the elevator ceiling as they make their way toward the Chancellor.

"My powers have doubled since we last met, Count." —Anakin

Super battle droids have a slippery time with R2-D2.

Can General Grievous keep Anakin, Palpatine, and Obi-Wan captive?

General Grievous: mostly droid, all evil!

The Jedi make a crash-landing.

Anakin wakes from a horrible nightmare.

Can Yoda help Anakin?

Can Palpatine?

Anakin and Padmé share their love . . . and their secret

Obi-Wan gets some information from Tion Medon on Utapau.

Obi-Wan and Grievous face off!

Saesee Tiin, Eeth Koth, Mace Windu, and Kit Fisto prepare to arrest the Chancellor.

Clone troopers turn against their Jedi generals on Felucia.

The Wookiees mount a defense on Kashyyyk . . .

. . . including a Wookiee named Chewbacca.

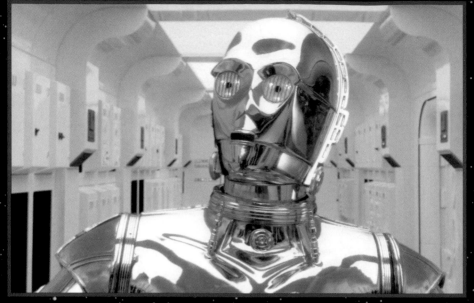

C-3PO knows there's trouble.

Anakin heads to Mustafar to destroy
the Separatist Council.

Betrayed by Anakin's turn to the dark side,
Obi-Wan must fight him in an epic battle.

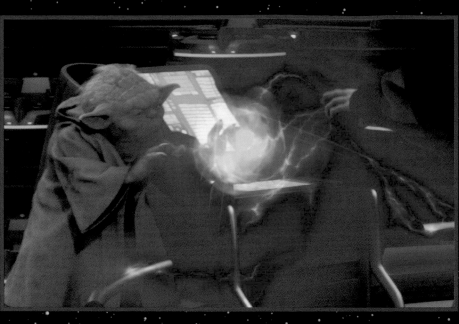

Don't mess with Yoda.

A Sith Lord is born: Darth Vader.

Obi-Wan gives baby Luke to Beru Lars.

The galaxy awaits the return of the Jedi.

Anakin nodded. Feeling much happier, Obi-Wan started down the ramp toward the clone troops. Then the full force of his own words hit him, and he realized that Anakin might be as worried about him as he was about Anakin. He turned.

"Don't worry," he told Anakin. "I have enough clones with me to take three systems the size of Utapau." He waved at the ranks of white-armored clones below, and smiled. "I think I'll be able to handle the situation — even without your help."

"Well, there's always a first time," Anakin replied. His grin seemed a little strained, but the teasing tone was pure mischief.

Obi-Wan laughed. "Good-bye, old friend. May the Force be with you."

"May the Force be with you," Anakin echoed. His voice was serious — almost somber.

As Obi-Wan walked toward the waiting starcruiser, uneasiness struck him. *This is just an ordinary mission*, he told himself. *I'll be back in a week or two. If something's bothering Anakin, we can talk about it then.*

But for some reason, he felt as if he'd said good-bye to his best friend and former apprentice for the last time.

Anakin stood watching until the last clone trooper boarded the starcruiser. Only when the ship took off did he leave the landing area. He felt empty and adrift, as if he'd lost an anchor. *And I never did get to talk to Obi-Wan about the Jedi Council.*

Without thinking about it, Anakin headed for Padmé's apartment. Though she had lived mainly on Coruscant for nearly ten years, her rooms held the peace and comfort of her home planet, Naboo. He needed that peace and comfort right now.

She still keeps the temperature too low, though, Anakin thought as he entered. He smiled. It was an old argument between them. His own home, Tatooine, was a desert planet, and although he had adjusted to the varying climates of planets all over the Republic, he still felt most comfortable when the air was warmer than most beings preferred.

Something in him relaxed as he called a greeting to Padmé and sat down to work on his report for the Council. This was what mattered: this place where he was always welcomed and loved. Where he could be himself, just Anakin Skywalker, eating and sleeping and kissing his wife like other, ordinary people. Home.

He heard Padmé enter the room behind him. With her came the faint traces of a familiar presence. Anakin lowered his datascanner. "Obi-Wan's been here, hasn't he?" he asked.

"He came by this morning," Padmé confirmed.

That must have been right before the Council meeting, Anakin thought. *Why didn't he say anything to me?* "What did he want?" he asked.

"He's worried about you."

Why would Obi-Wan come to Padmé if he was worried about Anakin? Unless — "You told him about us, didn't you?" Anakin couldn't keep the anger out of his voice.

Padmé glanced at him and walked on, into the bedroom. Anakin followed, waiting. Finally, she said, "He's your best friend, Anakin. He says you're under a lot of stress."

"And he's not?"

"You have been moody lately."

"I'm not moody!" He flung the words at her, wishing he could shout at Obi-Wan, too. *They're acting like I'm a child.*

"Anakin!" Padmé looked at him with a tired sadness that cut at his heart. "Don't do this again."

Anakin turned away, wondering how he could explain. *I killed a defenseless prisoner, against the Code. The Jedi Council asked me to spy on the Chancellor, also against the Jedi Code. The Chancellor says the Council wants to take over the Republic. The Council says the Chancellor has too much power. I don't know anymore who to believe or what to believe in. And I'm so afraid of losing you that I can't think straight and none of the rest of it matters.* "I don't know," he told her at last. "I feel . . . lost."

"Lost?" Padmé gazed at him in surprised concern. "You're always so sure of yourself. I don't understand."

"Obi-Wan and the Council don't trust me." *And I'm not sure I can trust them.*

Padmé shook her head. "They trust you with their lives. Obi-Wan loves you as a son."

Maybe Obi-Wan does. But he's gone, hunting General Grievous. He tried again. "Something's happening. I'm not the Jedi I should be." Padmé shook her head again, and he held up a hand to stop her. "I am one of the most powerful Jedi, but I'm not satisfied. I want more, but I know I shouldn't."

"You're only human, Anakin," Padmé told him gently. "No one expects any more."

Yes, they do. And I do. That was why Obi-Wan kept lecturing him about pride and ambition and jealousy — and that was why he hated those lectures so much. Because he knew Obi-Wan was right. A Jedi Knight shouldn't have those thoughts. Anakin closed his eyes. He should have known Padmé wouldn't understand. She wasn't a Jedi.

But she would be the mother of his child. Anakin felt a tingle of fear and excitement at the thought. "I have found a way to save you," he said.

"Save me?"

"From my nightmares." *Surely she hasn't forgotten!*

Padmé smiled slightly. "Is *that* what's bothering you?"

"I won't lose you, Padmé."

"I'm not going to die in childbirth, Anakin," she said quietly. "I promise you."

"No, *I* promise *you*!" Recklessly, he made the vow, though he did not yet have the power to fulfill it. Chancellor Palpatine might think that the story of Darth Plagueis was only a legend, but Anakin knew it was true. He could *feel* it. And if Darth Plagueis could discover the secret, so could he. There was time. "I will become powerful enough to keep you from dying."

Padmé caught his eyes and held them. "You don't need more power, Anakin," she said slowly and seriously. "I believe you can protect me against anything, just as you are."

And I will, Anakin thought as he gathered her into his arms. *I will protect you.* No matter what it takes.

CHAPTER 11

All the way to Utapau, Obi-Wan considered how best to find and destroy General Grievous. If they blasted their way in, Grievous would only run away again — the droid general was always careful to have an escape ship stashed somewhere close to his command center. He might not even be with his armies. His command center might be hidden in one part of the Utapau system, while his droids massed for an attack somewhere else.

So Obi-Wan decided to keep his clone troops in space aboard the Jedi cruiser and search the system himself, quietly. That way, he could be sure that when he told his forces to attack, they would be attacking the right place.

Commander Cody accepted the order without question, as he always did. The clones had been genetically engineered to take orders; that was why each major offensive needed a Jedi Knight as general. Though he had worked and fought with the clones for years, their willingness to follow any order, no matter how unreasonable, still made Obi-Wan uneasy. Free beings shouldn't be so . . . obedient.

Obi-Wan snorted. How many times had he complained about Anakin's independence and headstrong ways? And here he was, worried because his clone troops were *too* compliant. Anakin would laugh himself sick if he knew what his Master was thinking.

The planet of Utapau looked peaceful enough as Obi-Wan flew over it in his starfighter. He saw no sign of the droid armies. The huge sinkhole cities looked quiet. Well, he hadn't expected General Grievous to be out in plain sight, and Utapau *was* officially neutral. He'd have to refuel and search the rest of the system.

Arranging a landing was no problem. A worried-looking local administrator even came out to the ship to greet him. Obi-Wan bowed politely to him. "With your kind permission, I would like some fuel, and to use your city as a base to search nearby systems."

The administrator gestured, and a ground crew rushed out to service the fighter. "What are you searching for?" he asked as if it were of no particular interest.

"A droid army," Obi-Wan replied. "Led by General Grievous."

The Utapauan held very still for a moment. Then he leaned sideways, as if he were inspecting the underside of Obi-Wan's fighter. The movement brought his head close to Obi-Wan and hid his face from the windows above. Very quietly, he said, "Grievous is here! We are being held hostage. They are watching us."

"I understand," Obi-Wan replied just as softly. If he made the wrong move, the droids would slaughter thousands of civilians. No wonder the administrator was worried!

"The tenth level," the Utapauan whispered before he straightened up. Obi-Wan nodded and walked back to the starfighter. He made a show of ducking underneath it, to make it seem as if he were studying something the Utapaun had pointed out. Then he climbed back into the fighter.

As the ground crew finished its work, Obi-Wan set up a secure communication channel to his clone troops. "I have located General Grievous," he told the commander. "Report to the Jedi Council at once. I'm staying here."

He cut the signal, then gave a few quick instructions to his R4 unit and slipped out of the starfighter on the far side of the cockpit. By the time the fighter took off, he was hidden in the shadows at the entrance to the sinkhole city. *Now all I have to do is get to the tenth level and defeat Grievous.*

Getting there was actually much easier than he expected. The stairs were blocked and the elevators had been shut down, but no one had bothered to put a guard on the open walls of the sinkhole itself. All Obi-Wan had to do was find one of the giant lizards that the Utapauans used as riding beasts. The lizard climbed the sinkhole wall easily, and soon Obi-Wan was riding across the edge of the tenth level, searching for the control center.

He found it a quarter of the way around the sinkhole — the hordes of battle droids made it unmistakable, even if General Grievous himself hadn't been standing at the far end along with the members of the Separatist Council. That was an unexpected complication. He couldn't take on all of them — and all their formidable bodyguards — at once, not alone. Besides, if he could get close enough to hear what they were saying, he might find out some of their plans. He climbed down from the lizard and slipped along a high, narrow walkway, hoping the sound of their voices would carry once he got near enough.

General Grievous surveyed the Separatist Council with disgust — the Neimoidians, Nute Gunray and Rune Haako, who represented the Trade Federation; archduke Poggle the Lesser, who was oddly fierce-looking for a banker; Shu Mai, San Hill, Wat Tambor, and the rest. Not for the first time, Grievous was glad that his smooth metal face could show no emotion. It would be unfortunate if these beings realized how much contempt he had for them.

The Council stirred. If he let them start talking again, they'd be here all day. They'd already wasted too much time asking questions and solemnly discussing pointless alternatives. It was time to *make* them move. "It won't be long before the armies of the Republic track us here," Grievous told them bluntly. "Make your way to the Mustafar system in the Outer Rim. You will be safe there."

Nute Gunray goggled at Grievous. His large bulging eyes made him look vaguely froglike. "Safe?" he sputtered. "Chancellor Palpatine managed to escape your grip, General. I have doubts about your ability to keep us *safe*."

There was a murmur of agreement from the other councilors. Grievous drew himself up to his full height and thrust his head toward the indignant Neimoidian. "Be thankful, Viceroy, that you have not found *yourself* in my grip," he said in a low, menacing voice. Gunray shrank away, and the murmuring died abruptly. Grievous waited to be sure the lesson had sunk in. "Your ship is waiting," he told the group.

The Separatist Council could hardly wait to leave.

Grievous stood motionless and silently threatening as the Councilors hurried out, casting nervous backward glances in his direction. *It takes so little to frighten ordinary beings*, he thought. *And fear is so useful . . .*

Now all he had to do was stay on Utapau until that annoying Jedi fell into the trap. With luck, it wouldn't be a long wait.

When the Separatist Council filed out, Obi-Wan stayed motionless, hoping that some of the hundreds of battle droids would leave, too. None of them moved. *This is it, then.* Obi-Wan took just a moment longer, to center himself in the living Force. Then he took off his cloak and leaped down, landing lightly right in front of General Grievous.

The droid general's smooth metal face was impossible to read, but his tone was puzzled as he said, "I find your behavior bewildering. Surely you realize you're doomed."

"I've brought two full legions with me," Obi-Wan said. "And this time, you won't escape."

Grievous signaled, and his four bodyguards stepped forward, whirling their electro-staffs.

Obi-Wan ducked and ignited his lightsaber. He feinted, to keep the droids' attention on his weapon while he used the Force to drop a huge rectagular slab of durasteel down from the ceiling.

The tactic worked even better than he'd hoped. Three of the guards were crushed outright; the fourth was partially pinned, and was struggling to get at his electro-staff. Obi-Wan's lightsaber cut him neatly apart as he went past, heading for General Grievous.

More droids poured into the room, but General Grievous waved them off. He threw back his cloak, revealing the belt hung with the stolen lightsabers of the Jedi he'd killed. Reaching down, he took two in each hand. *What does he think he's doing?* Obi-Wan wondered, and then the general's metal arms split lengthwise, and Obi-Wan was facing a four-armed enemy with a lightsaber in each hand.

"Count Dooku trained me in the Jedi arts," Grievous said, and attacked. He spun two of the lightsabers like deadly buzzsaws, while he stabbed with the other two whenever he saw an opening.

It was almost like fighting four different people at once. Obi-Wan's lightsaber blurred as he blocked and parried, but he knew he couldn't keep that up for long. *Time for a different approach.* He leaped, flipping high over Grievous to land behind him.

Grievous didn't have to turn; he just rotated his mechanical body until he faced the other way. But even doing that took time and threw off his attack, just enough to let Obi-Wan's lightsaber swirl past his guard. Two of his four arms dropped to the floor, still gripping their stolen lightsabers.

Before Grievous could adjust, and attack with his

two remaining lightsabers, Obi-Wan reached for the Force. He lifted Grievous into the air, throwing him against one of the beams that supported the upper level. The impact shook the lightsabers out of his grasp. They landed on the floor of the control center, while Grievous slid past the edge of the floor and fell to the level below.

The room was filling up with blaster fire; the clone troopers had arrived and were keeping the battle droids busy. Obi-Wan rushed to the edge in time to see Grievous scuttle toward a one-man wheel scooter. *I knew it! He has an escape ship some-where, and he thinks he's going to get to it while these droids keep me busy! Well, not this time.*

In a fury of light, Obi-Wan sent a volley of shots back at the battle droids and whistled for his riding lizard, just as the general kicked his scooter into motion and roared away. The lizard jumped down, landing on a battle droid. Obi-Wan leaped onto the lizard's back, and took off after Grievous.

Anakin frowned as he hurried through the halls of the Senate Office building. It should be good news that he was bringing to Chancellor Palpatine, but the way Master Windu talked during the Jedi Council meeting had made him uneasy. *The clone comman-der said that Obi-Wan has found General Grievous.* The hologram transmission had, for once, been perfectly clear, with none of the wavering and static caused by jammers or other interference. Anakin had even seen the clone troopers in the background, preparing for the assault.

He'd expected the other Council members to be elated. Instead, they'd looked grave and made ambiguous remarks about watching the Chancellor's reaction to the news. *The war is going to be over soon. Of course he'll be happy! What else are they expecting?*

But Chancellor Palpatine received the news with the same serious expression as the Council members had. "Finding this droid general is not the same as defeating him," Palpatine murmured. "We can only hope that Master Kenobi is up for the challenge."

"I should be there with him," Anakin said.

"It upsets me that the Council doesn't fully appreciate your talents," the Chancellor went on. "Don't you wonder why they wouldn't make you a Jedi Master?"

"I wish I knew." Anakin shook his head. "I know there are things about the Force that they are not telling me."

"They don't trust you, Anakin." Palpatine paused. "They want to take control of the Senate."

"That's not true," Anakin said automatically. Jedi didn't want power. *But if the Jedi Council doesn't care about power, why are they so worried about the Chancellor?*

"Are you sure? What if I am right, and they are plotting to take over the Republic?" Chancellor Palpatine shook his head in mild exasperation. "Anakin! Break through the fog of lies the Jedi have created. I am your friend. Let me help you to learn the true ways of the Force."

Anakin felt a cold chill. Palpatine wasn't a Jedi. "How do you know the ways of the Force?"

"My mentor taught me everything," Palpatine replied calmly. "Even the nature of the dark side."

"You know the dark side?" Anakin stopped short as the sense of the words crashed down onto him. "You're a Sith Lord!" he said, and ignited his lightsaber.

CHAPTER 12

Chancellor Palpatine, whose Sith name was Darth Sidious, looked calmly at the angry young Jedi with the glowing lightsaber. This was the point toward which all his plots and plans had been heading for many years. "Yes, I am a Sith Lord," he told Anakin. As Anakin raised his lightsaber, Palpatine added gently, "And I am also the one who has held this Republic together during these troubled times. I am not your enemy, Anakin."

He could sense Anakin's growing confusion, and suppressed a smile. These Jedi expected all Sith Lords to be like those apprentices of his, Darth Maul and Darth Tyranus — ready to whip out a lightsaber the moment they were discovered. But a lightsaber was such an *obvious* weapon. Words were better. All you could do with a lightsaber was kill the man you faced. With words, you could change his mind, so that he would help you instead of fighting you. That was *true* power.

And Anakin was listening to him. Time, now, to begin the final stage that would turn Anakin to the dark side at last. Palpatine let his tone fall into lecturing. "Anakin, if one is to understand a great mystery, one must study all aspects of it, not just the dogmatic, narrow view of the Jedi. If you wish to become a complete and wise leader, you must embrace a larger view of the Force."

He paused, to give his words time to sink in. Then, in a deliberately different tone, he went on. "Be careful of the Jedi, Anakin. They fear you. In time, they will destroy you." He put pleading into his voice, like the kindly uncle he had pretended to be for so long. "Let me train you, Anakin. I will show you the true nature of the Force."

Palpatine could see Anakin considering it, but then Anakin shook his head. "I won't be a pawn in your political game, Chancellor. The Jedi are my family."

There *had* to be a way to shake that confidence of his — ah, yes. "Only through me can you achieve a power greater than any Jedi. Learn to control the dark side of the Force, Anakin, and you will be able to save Padmé from certain death."

"W-what are you talking about?"

"I know what has been troubling you," Palpatine said gently. "Listen to me. Use my knowledge, I beg you!"

"I won't become a Sith!" But Anakin's denial was

too passionate, as if he was trying to convince himself as much as Palpatine. "I should kill you!"

But you haven't killed me, have you, my fine young Jedi? You were already wondering about the truth of those overly simple Jedi teachings, and now I'm not acting the way you think a Sith Lord should. A little more, and you'll join me — perhaps not this minute, but soon. When you've had time to calm down and think.

But I must move slowly, Palpatine reminded himself. A misstep could still spoil all his careful work. "Of course you should," Palpatine agreed. "Except for the fact that we are both working for the same goal — a more perfect future for the Republic."

"You have deceived everyone!"

"A painful necessity." What had the boy expected him to do — begin by announcing to the entire galaxy that he was one of the feared and hated Sith Lords, and *then* try to get elected Chancellor? "The Republic was rotting from within. The system had to be shaken to its core. Yet no one, not the Senate, not the courts, not even the Jedi Council, could do anything. I was the only one who dared to clean up the mess." The old anger and conviction shook him as he spoke, and he felt Anakin's reaction to the truth of his words.

He paused. *Time to let him think*. Palpatine made a show of studying Anakin's lightsaber. "Are you going to kill me?" he asked calmly, as though it were a minor matter of curiosity.

"I would certainly like to," Anakin growled.

"I know you would." Palpatine allowed himself a smile as he turned away. "I can *feel* your anger. It gives you *focus*, makes you *stronger*. The question is, will you kill me if it means plunging the galaxy into eternal chaos and strife?"

Anakin lifted his lightsaber. Palpatine kept his expression relaxed and disinterested. *If I've pushed him too far, too fast . . .* But Anakin did not complete the movement. At last, he lowered the lightsaber and said, "I am going to turn you over to the Jedi Council."

"But you're not sure of their intentions, are you?" Palpatine almost smiled again as Anakin's eyes slid away from his. He would win this contest, after all. "I want you to meditate on my proposal," he said coolly. "Know the power of the dark side. The power to save Padmé."

Anakin stared at him for a long moment, then finally turned off his lightsaber. As if nothing unusual had happened, Palpatine walked to his desk and sat down. Seeing the surprise in Anakin's eyes, he said, "I am not going anywhere. You have time to decide my fate." *And to think about my offer.*

As Anakin turned and all but ran from the room, Palpatine added softly, "Perhaps you'll reconsider, and help me rule the galaxy. For the good of all."

Anakin's Jedi senses would hear that final whisper. His ambition would bring him back to Palpatine, if his fear for Padmé didn't.

And then, once more, there would be two Sith Lords, Master and apprentice.

Ruling the galaxy, for a thousand years.

General Grievous is an even more reckless driver than Anakin, Obi-Wan observed as his lizard raced through the tunnel city after the general's wheel scooter. Blaster fire from clone troops and battle droids filled the air, and there were explosions everywhere — not to mention armored transports full of droids and clones. The scooter hurtled through them as if they weren't there, narrowly avoiding crash after crash and crushing those in its way. Obi-Wan's lizard was having a hard time keeping up.

A stray laser blast whizzed past Obi-Wan's ear, and he reached for his lightsaber. It wasn't there. *It must have been knocked loose right after I jumped on the lizard,* Obi-Wan thought. *I hope Anakin never hears about this.* But now he had to guide the lizard so that they avoided the shots, instead of just deflecting them. They lost ground.

As they moved farther into the city, the tunnels became more crowded. Obi-Wan lost more ground as he wove through the battling droids and vehicles. The crowd was slowing Grievous down, too; Obi-Wan saw Grievous' scooter roll up onto the curving walls to get around a mob of battle droids running up the tunnel toward them.

Obi-Wan smiled suddenly. His lizard could do things the general's scooter couldn't. He urged the lizard up onto the wall, and then to the ceiling. The lizard used its natural abilities to cling upside down, and Obi-Wan used the Force to cling to the lizard. Nobody else was using the ceiling as a highway, so they didn't lose any more time dodging traffic. They gained on Grievous rapidly.

Ahead, Obi-Wan could see the tunnel opening out into a small landing platform. He dug his heels into the lizard, which leaped forward. He was next to Grievous now, close enough to strike at him, if he'd only had his lightsaber. Unfortunately, Grievous hadn't dropped his electro-staff, and he was close enough to strike at Obi-Wan.

As the staff swung at him, Obi-Wan grabbed it and yanked hard, throwing Grievous off balance. Calling on the Force, he leaped from his lizard to tackle the general. The tactic worked; Obi-Wan and Grievous fell to the floor of the landing platform together, and the electro-staff went flying.

General Grievous did not spare a glance for the missing staff. He pulled out a blaster. Obi-Wan grabbed for it, and it, too, went flying out of reach. Obi-Wan rolled and grabbed the electro-staff. It wasn't as good as a lightsaber, but it would do.

His first blow caught General Grievous squarely in his midsection. Obi-Wan swung again and connected with one of the general's arms. The metal arm bent, but did not break. An instant later, too fast for even Jedi reflexes to avoid, Grievous' other arm struck Obi-Wan.

It was like being hit with a metal construction bar. Obi-Wan's shoulder and half his side went numb, then flared into pain. The electro-staff went flying once more, and he barely dodged the next blow. *That was brutal! I'd better not let him catch me with any more of those.*

Using the Force, Obi-Wan leaped, putting all his weight and momentum behind his kick. Grievous hardly seemed to notice it. His metal limbs and the durasteel shell that encased his body were tougher than those of any droid Obi-Wan had ever faced.

There must be some way to get at him! Obi-Wan dodged another swing, and saw a corner of Grievous' stomach plate shift as the droid general moved. *It must have been loosened when I hit him with the electro-staff. Maybe I can get some of that armor off of him . . .*

As the general swung again, Obi-Wan ducked and closed in. He grabbed the loose corner and pulled. The plate came free — and the general's metal arms closed around Obi-Wan and lifted him high. Then he was flying through the air, to land heavily on the far side of the platform. Half-stunned, he slid across the surface and almost over the edge. At the last minute, he grabbed hold, stopping with his legs dangling above the long, long drop to the bottom of the sinkhole.

Dimly, Obi-Wan saw General Grievous pick up the electro-staff and start toward him. He struggled back to full consciousness, thinking, *I need a weapon!*

Then he saw the general's abandoned blaster, lying a few yards away.

Barely in time, he called the blaster to him, and fired. General Grievous stopped moving forward. Obi-Wan poured shot after shot into the general's open stomach area. The half-droid made a sound that was part choking noise, part metallic screech, and then there was a small explosion inside his metal body.

Holding the laser pistol ready, Obi-Wan watched as more explosions shook the cyborg general's metal casing. Finally, flames burst from his eye slits, and General Grievous collapsed in a smoking heap. Obi-Wan reached out with the Force, to sense any flicker of remaining life.

He found none. Heaving a sigh of relief, he started back toward the tunnel to recapture his lizard, and realized he was still holding the laser pistol. He looked at it with distaste. *So uncivilized!*

Tossing it over the edge of the landing platform, Obi-Wan went to see how the battle was going. He didn't really have any doubts. Clone Commander Cody was competent, and he had more than enough troops to handle the battle droids. General Grievous had been the real problem, and that was taken care of.

All that's left is to notify the Council — and the Chancellor. And then . . . then we'll find out the Chancellor's real intentions.

When Anakin finally found Master Windu in the Jedi Temple hangar, his head was still spinning. Master Windu and three other Jedi were preparing to board a gunship, and at first, he was not at all pleased by Anakin's interruption.

"What is it, Skywalker?" Master Windu snapped. "We are in a hurry. We've just received word that Obi-Wan has destroyed General Grievous. We are on our way to make sure the Chancellor gives his emergency powers back to the Senate."

"He won't give up his power," Anakin said heavily. He felt Master Windu's attention focus on him, and swallowed hard. "Chancellor Palpatine is a Sith Lord."

"A Sith Lord?" Master Windu sounded as horrified as Anakin had been. "How do you know this?"

He told me himself. "He knows the ways of the Force. He has been trained to use the dark side."

Master Windu stared at him for a long moment. At last he nodded. "Then our worst fears have been realized. We must move fast if the Jedi are to remain in control."

As Master Windu signaled the other Jedi to board the gunship, Anakin said, "Master, the Chancellor is very powerful." He hesitated. "You will need my help if you are going to arrest him."

Mace Windu's eyes narrowed. "For your own good, you stay out of this conflict," he commanded sternly. "I sense much confusion in you, young Sky-walker. Your fear clouds your judgment."

"That's not true, Master," Anakin protested.

"We'll see," Mace responded. "If what you say is true, you will have earned my trust. For now, you *stay here*. Wait for us in the Council Chamber until we return."

He still doesn't trust me. He never has. But Mace Windu was a senior Council member, a Master. As long as Anakin was a Jedi, he had to follow Master Windu's orders. "Yes, Master," he said, trying to keep the resentment out of his voice.

Mace nodded once, and entered the gunship. Anakin stayed where he was until the gunship took off, hoping until the last minute that Mace would change his mind. When the ship finally vanished into the endless stream of traffic, he turned and went back into the Jedi Temple.

The Council Chamber was dim and empty. Anakin sat in one of the chairs and tried to meditate, but his mind and heart were in too much turmoil. Now that he was alone, his mission accomplished, the Chancellor's words kept replaying in his mind. *Learn to control the dark side of the Force, and you will be able to save Padmé from certain death.* Anakin felt cold, remembering the screams that echoed through his dreams. Again, he heard Padmé's dying cry: "Anakin! I love you."

The Chancellor's voice spoke in his mind, words he had *not* said before: "You do know that if the Jedi destroy me, any chance of saving Padmé will be lost."

No! Anakin reached out blindly, not to the Chancellor, but to the one he loved. To Padmé. And then he sensed her presence, as if she were there, not just in the Jedi Council Chamber, but in his own mind and heart — a true joining through the Force.

Padmé was alone in the central room of her apartment, when she felt Anakin's presence in the room with her. *What is he doing here at this hour?* she thought, and looked up. She blinked and shook her head. The room was empty, but just for an instant she thought she had seen the Jedi Council Chamber.

And then the connection took hold fully, and she knew. Anakin was there, alone in the Council

Chamber — and he was here, too, with her. She felt his love, and his fear for her — the terrible fear that was eating at his heart. The fear that she would die. She hadn't known how terrible his fear was.

I am not afraid to die. She'd told him that once, when they were being led into the arena on Geonosis for execution, and it was still true. She was only afraid that he would not know how much she loved him. As the Force connection began to fade, she spoke again the words she had said then, when she first declared her love for him. Anakin wouldn't hear them, of course, but perhaps he would feel the love behind them, the love that was stronger and deeper now than it had ever been.

"I truly, deeply love you," Padmé's voice said in Anakin's mind. *"Before I die, I want you to know."*

The last of the Force connection faded, but her words echoed: *Before I die, before I die, before I die.* Anakin shuddered. *Padmé, no!* But the link was gone, she was gone, and he was alone in the Council Chamber. As he would be alone, always and everywhere, once Padmé was dead.

"No!" The word tore from his lips. He was on his feet, panting as if he had been running. *I can't do this! I can't let her die!* And then he *was* running, out of the Council Chamber toward the platform where his airspeeder was parked.

The trip to the Senate Office building seemed to take forever. Anakin was vaguely aware of other traffic dodging and beeping at him, and of the gauges on his control panel all pushing into the red zone. Then he was running through the halls toward the hum of a lightsaber in the Chancellor's office.

He stopped in the doorway, shocked motionless. Wind whistled past him from the gaping hole that had been the huge window overlooking Coruscant. Shards of glass littered the floor and dusted across three crumpled figures in Jedi robes. Only one Jedi still stood — Mace Windu, his purple lightsaber menacing Chancellor Palpatine. "You're under arrest, my lord," he told the Chancellor, motioning to Anakin to stay back.

But Palpatine was not looking at Mace Windu. "Anakin!" he cried. "I told you it would come to this. I was right. The Jedi are taking over."

But . . . but . . . That's not right. They came here because I told them you were a Sith Lord, not in order to take over. But they'd already been on their way to arrest Palpatine when he arrived with the news, a different part of Anakin thought.

"Your plot to regain control of the Republic is over," Master Windu said. "You have *lost.*"

"No!" Palpatine raised his hands. "*You* will die!" Blue Force lightning shot from his fingers toward Mace.

Anakin took an involuntary step forward. "He is a

traitor, Anakin!" Palpatine cried as more lightning poured from his hands.

"He's the traitor!" Mace said. He grimaced with the effort of repelling the lightning. "Stop him!"

Anakin's head swiveled from one man to the other. The Force lightning was hurting Master Windu now, hurting him badly. But the Chancellor was aging before Anakin's eyes. His hair thinned and his skin shriveled. Deep furrows appeared in his forehead. His hands twisted and turned gray-white. "Help me!" he cried. "I can't hold on any longer."

But Anakin stayed frozen. At last Palpatine collapsed, exhausted. "I give up," he said in the whispery voice of an old, old man. "I am . . . I am too weak. Don't kill me. I give up."

Mace Windu pointed his lightsaber at the cringing Chancellor. "You Sith disease," he snarled. "I am going to end this right now."

"You can't kill him, Master," Anakin protested. "He must stand trial."

"He has too much control over the Senate and the Courts," Mace replied. "He is too dangerous to be kept alive."

"It's not the Jedi way." But the Chancellor had said the same thing about Count Dooku. If Jedi Master and Sith Lord made the same argument, were they really so different? *And I need him to save Padmé.*

But Master Windu wasn't listening. He raised his

lightsaber — and Anakin knocked it aside. The unexpected blow sent the lightsaber flying . . . and left Mace defenseless against a new bolt of Force lightning. *Chancellor Palpatine was faking! He wasn't tired at all.*

Mace howled and retreated. "Power!" the Chancellor cried, and laughed. "Absolute power!"

Another wave of Force lightning struck Mace and slammed him backward, and back again, then it lifted him through the space where the window had been, high into the night sky — and then let him drop the hundreds of meters to the ground below. Anakin stared after him, horrified. "What have I done?" he whispered.

"You are fulfilling your destiny," Palpatine replied calmly. He looked different now, and sounded different. The aging was no illusion. But the difference made it easier for Anakin to be different himself. To say what he knew he had come to say.

"I will do whatever you ask," he told Palpatine. "Just help me save Padmé's life." *I can't live without her. I won't let her die.*

Palpatine smiled and gestured. Anakin knelt before him, and the words came — the words he had used to pledge to the Jedi, but changed, as he had changed. "I pledge myself to your care," he said. "To the ways of the Sith."

"Anakin Skywalker, you are one with the Order of

the Sith Lords," Palpatine replied. "Henceforth, you shall be known as . . . Darth Vader."

"Thank you, my Master."

Darth Sidious — Chancellor Palpatine — stood alone in his enormous office. He'd sent his new apprentice and a battalion of clone troops to the Jedi Temple. That would take care of the Jedi on Coruscant. He scowled slightly under his hood. He sensed that his apprentice was not yet as fully committed to the dark side as he should be. Well, destroying the Jedi here should certainly tie Anakin closer to his Sith identity — Darth Vader.

Now it was time to deal with the rest of the Jedi. The frown vanished, replaced by a smile of anticipation. Reaching out, he keyed a frequency into his hologram projector, and waited.

A small hologram of the first of the clone commanders sprang up before him. "Yes, my lord?"

"The time has come," Darth Sidious said, savoring the words. *After a thousand years, the time for revenge has come at last.* "Execute Order Sixty-six."

"I understand, my lord," the clone commander replied, and the image winked out.

Darth Sidious keyed in the next frequency, and another, identical hologram appeared. Again and again, he repeated the same words to clone commander after clone commander, on world after world. With every message, his faint smile grew.

The clone troops followed orders. That was, supposedly, why each battalion was led by a Jedi. What the Jedi had forgotten was that the clones served the Republic, not the Jedi Temple . . . and he, Darth Sidious, was the Supreme Chancellor of the Republic. The clones would follow the Chancellor's orders unquestioningly. Even if they were ordered to kill their Jedi leaders.

Order Sixty-six commanded the clones to do just that.

Still smiling, Darth Sidious leaned back, picturing the scenes all over the galaxy. Jedi on jungle planets, crystal worlds, water worlds, in the heat of battle and safe in their command centers, all dying at the hands of their own clone troops. He could sense it happening, though not in detail — but he could feel the dark side growing stronger with every Jedi death.

His only regret was that he couldn't be there in person to watch each one of them die.

CHAPTER 14

The trouble with droids is that they can't think, Obi-Wan told himself as he hacked his way through the battle droids that still clogged the sinkhole tunnel city on Utapau. An army made up of living beings would have seen how badly outnumbered they were, and given up. The droids just kept on fighting.

At least he had his lightsaber back. One of the clones had found it and returned it. *I'd hate to have to fight battle droids with nothing but a laser pistol*, Obi-Wan thought. He guided his lizard up the wall of the sinkhole, to get a better angle. *These droids —*

Suddenly, Obi-Wan felt a peculiar tremor in the Force, and started to turn his lizard. The lizard shifted just enough that the sudden intense blast of laser fire didn't destroy both it and Obi-Wan, but only knocked them off the wall of the sinkhole. As he made the long fall to the bottom of the sinkhole, Obi-Wan saw that the laser fire had come from *his own troops*. The clones were trying to kill him! *I have a bad feeling about this,* he thought, and hit the stagnant water below.

More laser blasts hit the surface of the water. Obi-Wan let the momentum of his fall carry him deep down, far below the level the blasts could reach. He fumbled at his belt pack for a moment before he found his breath mask and put it on. Now he could stay underwater until the clones gave up.

It took them a long time. No one could say clones weren't persistent but at last they must have assumed the great fall had killed him.

Fortunately the clones didn't know about General Grievous' little escape ship. Obi-Wan had only told them that Grievous was dead; there hadn't been time to go into details. *If I can get to that ship, I can get away. It's a Trade Federation model — even if the cruisers in orbit spot it, they'll think I'm a Separatist running away from the battle.* Of course, he'd still have to sneak past thousands of clone troops to get to the secret landing platform, but at least the clones wouldn't be waiting for him when he got there.

And once he was away from Utapau, he could find out what was going on. The clones weren't supposed to be *able* to betray the Republic. Something was very, very wrong.

The battle for Kashyyyk was over. Outside, the clones and Wookiees were picking up bits of smashed battle droids and repairing their own equipment. Yoda had left them to it. The clones did not need a commander to show them how to clean up debris, and the Wookiee meeting hall was quiet — a fine place to meditate. Chewbacca and Tarfful, the two Wookiee commanders, stayed to one side, and the clone officers kept near the entrance where they could keep an eye on the troops outside, and where any incoming messages would not disturb their commander.

Centuries of practice had made it easy for Yoda to slip his mind nearly free from his body, to rest in the living Force. Lately, he had taken the opportunity to do so whenever it arose. For as the dark side grew stronger over the years, so had his belief that someone was trying to reach him through the increasing gloom.

Eyes closed, Yoda gave himself up to the Force. Yes, there it was — the sense of someone reaching for him. Almost, he succeeded. Something brushed close to Yoda . . . no, some*one*, someone who felt familiar. And then, suddenly, shock waves ripped through the Force. *Jedi are dying.*

Yoda's eyes popped open. Two clone officers were coming up behind him. *To consult me, they pretend they are coming.* But Yoda could sense the faint aura of the dark side clinging to them. Something was very wrong, indeed.

So he was not surprised when the two clones

reached for their weapons. His lightsaber hummed in his hands, and an instant later two white-helmeted heads fell one way, and two bodies the other.

More, there will be. The clone officers would not have acted without orders, and a thousand more clones waited outside. Help, he must seek.

Fortunately, help was close at hand. The two Wookiees had seen the whole thing, and they recovered quickly from their surprise. Yoda explained what he needed, and the Wookiees nodded and exchanged comments in their barking language. Then Chewbacca picked Yoda up, and he and Tarfful retreated. They took Yoda out a back way, not a moment too soon. Seconds after they left it, a clone tank fired from a low hill nearby, and the meeting hall disappeared in a ball of fire.

It took the clones a little time to discover that Yoda had not been inside the hall when it blew up, but as soon as they did, they spread out in a search pattern, hunting for him. By then, the Wookiees had hidden him on one of the small boats. But he couldn't stay in hiding here. Too dangerous, it was, both for him and for the Wookiees. Besides, he had to get off the planet to find out what was happening.

When he told them the problem, the Wookiees nodded and barked at each other so fast that it was difficult even for him to follow the conversation. Then they turned and offered him one of their escape pods. Yoda accepted at once. The only problem left was how to get past the clone troops to the pod.

Senator Bail Organa was in an uneasy frame of mind as he flew his sleek airspeeder through the dawn light. Rumors had been flying around the Senate since early the previous evening. At first, the rumors were good — the Separatists had given up, the war was over, the Jedi had killed General Grievous. But before any of the rumors could be confirmed, new and frightening ones took their place — stories of rebellion, treason, murder, and betrayal. Bail didn't believe any of them, but they had grown and spread throughout the night. Finally, he had decided to see for himself just what was going on.

The first thing he saw was a cloud of black smoke billowing upward from the Jedi Temple. As he drew nearer, he saw white-clad clone troopers everywhere. *Where are the Jedi? Did the Separatists attack the Temple?*

No one seemed to be actually shooting, so Bail decided to land. Perhaps he could find out more. He picked a landing platform near the Temple entrance. Four clones stood guard in the doorway, but they lowered their weapons when they saw his Senatorial robes. "Don't worry, sir," one of them said. "The situation is under control."

"What's going on?" Bail asked, trying to sound casual instead of desperately anxious to know.

"There has been a rebellion, sir."

A rebellion? The smoke and the clone guards suddenly took on a new, sinister meaning. *The Jedi rebelled? Or . . . the clones? This doesn't make sense!* "That's impossible!"

"Don't worry, sir," the clone said again. "The situation is under control."

Bail frowned and started toward the Temple doors. As long as it was safe, he'd just go in and see for himself. But the clones blocked his path. "I'm sorry sir. No one is allowed entry." The clone paused, and to Bail's surprise and dismay, raised his blaster rifle. "It's time for you to leave, sir," he said pointedly.

Reluctantly, Bail turned back toward his speeder. It wouldn't do any good to get himself killed — and he didn't want to find out whether the clone troops really would fire on a Senator.

Just as he reached the speeder, he heard shots. Turning, he saw a boy, no more than ten years old, wearing Jedi robes and a desperate expression. He held a lightsaber, and the clone troops were shooting at him!

As Bail stared in horror, one of the clones looked up from the fight and pointed straight at him. "Take care of him," the clone told the four who had been guarding the door, and then he went back to the fight.

Bail leaped over his speeder an instant before the laser bolts started crashing around him. But the speeder wasn't armored; the clones would destroy it — and Bail — in a few moments, once they concentrated their fire. His only hope was to get away.

More clones were pouring out of the Jedi Temple; the Jedi boy must have been cut down. Angrily, Bail set the speeder in motion. A few stray shots followed him, but then the clones turned and went back inside the Temple. *Why should they bother with me? I'm not a Jedi.*

On the flight back to his office, Bail had a little time to think. Clone troops didn't act without orders, and there was only one person who could have ordered them to attack the Jedi Temple. Chancellor Palpatine. And Palpatine didn't leave loose ends. He must have some plan for disposing of the other Jedi who were off-planet. Also, Bail himself would become a loose end, if Palpatine heard about his visit to the Temple. Of course, Bail hadn't told the clones his name; if they hadn't recognized him, the Chancellor would never know. But Bail wasn't foolish enough to depend on that.

Bail flipped his communicator on and snapped orders. By the time he got back to his office, his two aides had packed up his most vital papers and were ready to go. There was one bad moment when two of the Chancellor's red-robed guards stopped them and demanded identification, but they were satisfied with his Senatorial ID card. Still, Bail's shoulders sagged in relief when he and his aides boarded the Alderaan starcruiser.

Captain Antilles, his pilot, was already on board with the rest of the crew. Bail wasted no time on pleasantries. "Were you able to get hold of a Jedi homing beacon?" he demanded.

"Yes, sir," Captain Antilles replied. "We've encountered no opposition. The clones are still a bit confused."

That's not surprising, if they've killed off all their Jedi commanders. Bail shuddered at the thought. He knew the confusion wouldn't last long — but at least it had lasted long enough for them to get away from Coruscant.

Bail gave the signal for the starcruiser to take off. They had the homing beacon; there was no more reason to stay. *Hopefully, we can intercept a few Jedi before they walk into this . . . catastrophe,* he thought as the ship left the atmosphere. He refused to think about just how few Jedi might be left to answer his bootleg beacon.

CHAPTER 15

Padmé heard the sound of a vehicle outside and hurried onto the veranda. A stab of relief made her head swim when she saw that it was a Jedi starfighter — and Anakin was climbing out of the cockpit onto the veranda stairs. "Are you all right?" she demanded, needing to hear it even though she could see that he was well. "I heard there was an attack on the Jedi Temple. You can see the smoke from here."

"I'm fine," Anakin said. His deep voice was tired; there was an edge to it, and to the way he moved. "I came to see if you and the baby are safe."

"Captain Typho's here," Padmé assured him. "We're safe. What's happening?" Behind them, she heard C-3PO asking R2-D2 the same question.

"The situation is not good," Anakin said heavily. "The Jedi Council has tried to overthrow the Republic."

Padmé stared at him in utter shock. He wasn't

joking; she could see that he wasn't joking. "I can't believe that!" she said at last.

"I couldn't either, at first," Anakin told her. "But it's true. I saw Master Windu attempt to assassinate the Chancellor myself."

How? How can this be? Padmé found a chair and sat down, stunned. "What are *you* going to do?" she asked at last.

"I will not betray the Republic," Anakin said. He swallowed. "My loyalties lie with the Chancellor and with the Senate. And with you."

With me, yes; I believe that. Padmé could hear the sincerity in his voice when he said that, and she had never doubted his loyalty to her. But there had been something odd in his tone when he spoke of the Chancellor and the Senate. Anakin had never cared much for politics. He cared about people, about Padmé and — "What about Obi-Wan?"

Anakin turned away so that she couldn't see his face. "I don't know," he said. "Many of the Jedi have been killed."

Not Obi-Wan! But . . . "Is he part of the rebellion?" Padmé asked hesitantly, though she wasn't sure she really wanted to know the answer.

"We may never know," Anakin said.

"How could this have happened?" Padmé asked. She looked up, and saw Anakin against the cityscape. The dawn sky was red and smoky — smoky from the burning Jedi Temple, as it had been smoky for days after the Separatist attack. Everyone kept saying that the war was almost over, yet the violence kept growing. "I want to leave," she said suddenly. "Go someplace far from here."

"Why?" Anakin sounded genuinely puzzled. "Things are different now. There is a new order."

Things are too different. War and death and betrayal are everywhere. My friends in the Senate are near to treason, and I'm not sure they're wrong. And I can't talk to you about it because it would be your job to arrest them. And maybe me. "I want to bring up our child somewhere safe," she said, and realized in some surprise that she had summed up everything she felt in one sentence.

"I want that, too," Anakin said. "But that place is here."

No, it isn't. Can't you see how dangerous Coruscant has become? But Anakin was a fighter; he'd been away at war for months. Coruscant probably did seem calm and peaceful to him, after all that.

"I'm gaining new knowledge of the Force," Anakin went on. *Soon I will be able to protect you from anything!*"

Padmé reached out to him. "Oh, Anakin, I'm afraid." *Afraid for our child. Afraid for the Republic. Afraid for myself. Afraid for you.*

"Have faith, my love," Anakin said, taking her into his arms. "Everything will soon be set right. The

Separatists have gathered in the Mustafar system. I'm going there to end this war."

Padmé shook her head wordlessly. How many times had they heard that doing this, winning that, killing the other, would end the war? And the war went on. She couldn't believe in the end of the war anymore.

"Wait until I return," Anakin begged. "Things will be different, I promise." He kissed her, long and lingering. "Please, wait for me."

She couldn't believe in the end of the war, but she could still believe in Anakin. "I will," Padmé said, and hugged him.

Anakin smiled in relief, and gave her a careful hug in return. Then, reluctantly, his arms dropped and he looked over at his fighter. With equal reluctance, Padmé let him go. As he climbed into the fighter, she felt tears sting her eyes, but she refused to let them fall. Anakin still had a job to do, and she wouldn't keep him from it, though she wanted so much to have more time with him.

C-3PO backed away, waving to R2-D2. The fighter took off. As it flew into the blood-red dawn, Padmé let the tears come. She felt more alone than she ever had in her life, and she didn't understand why. After all, she still had Anakin.

Sneaking through the Utapauan tunnels to General Grievous' hidden starfighter was not just a matter of dodging the clone troops that crowded the stairs and tunnels. Obi-Wan had commanded these clones; he knew the search patterns they would use and which areas they were most likely to inspect first. But the tunnels were home to a number of unfriendly Utapaun creatures, some of which were large and hungry as well as unfriendly. Several times Obi-Wan had to fight his way past them.

When he finally reached the tiny landing platform, he was relieved to see that the clones had not yet discovered the ship. The whole area was as deserted as it had been when he had chased General Grievous into it. Hardly daring to believe his luck, he slipped into the fighter. No laser blasts flared. He studied the controls briefly, then set the ship in motion.

Obi-Wan flew low, hugging the surface of Utapau, until he was well away from the sinkhole city and the masses of clone troops and transports. The clones wouldn't expect to find Obi-Wan in a Trade Federation fighter, but they might shoot it down all the same. The Separatists were still the enemy — at least, the few times Obi-Wan had seen clone troops in the Utapau tunnels, they had still been fighting Separatist battle droids. There was no reason to take extra chances.

On the far side of Utapau, Obi-Wan headed into space. As soon as he was out of scanning range, he activated the fighter's comm and punched in the main Jedi communication frequency. To his surprise, all he got was static.

Frowning, he tried another frequency, with the same result. And another. Finally, he set the comm to scan. After a minute, it began beeping steadily. *A Jedi homing beacon! But there aren't supposed to be any other Jedi out here.* He picked up his comlink.

"Emergency Code Nine Thirteen," Obi-Wan said. "I have no contact on any frequency. Are there any Jedi out there? Anywhere?"

A wavering hologram image appeared above the comm. Quickly, Obi-Wan locked on to the signal, and the image steadied. To his surprise, it was Senator Bail Organa of Alderaan. *What's he doing with a Jedi homing beacon?*

"Master Kenobi?" The Senator sounded pleased to see him, at least.

"Senator Organa," Obi-Wan said. "My clone troops turned on me. I need help."

Bail Organa did not look surprised, and his next words explained why. "We have just rescued Master Yoda," he said. "It appears this ambush has happened everywhere. Lock onto my coordinates."

Darth Sidious looked at the incoming message coordinates and frowned slightly. Mustafar? He hadn't been expecting a transmission from that planet yet. Had something gone wrong? He pressed the response button, and a blue hologram appeared. It was a Neimoidian — the Trade Federation viceroy, Nute

Gunray. *My apprentice has not yet reached Mustafar, then.*

Gunray bowed deeply. Behind him, Darth Sidious could see the rest of the Separatist Council. "The plan has gone as you had promised, my lord," the Neimoidian told him.

"You have done well, Viceroy," Darth Sidious responded automatically. "Have you shut down your droid armies?"

"We have, my lord."

He smiled. "Excellent! Has my new apprentice, Darth Vader, arrived?"

"He landed a few moments ago," Gunray replied.

"Good, good. He will take care of you." The ambiguity of the words pleased him. He reached for the controls, to end the transmission, and paused.

The transparent blue faces all turned to look at something outside the range of the hologram pickup. Their expressions changed from surprise to bewilderment, and then to fear. Darth Sidious leaned forward in anticipation.

A glowing lightsaber slashed across the pickup field. A head fell one way — Poggle the Lesser, Sidious noted — and the body the other. The rest of the Separatist Council shook off their stupor and fled, screaming, as the transmission cut off at the other end.

"I see my apprentice has arrived," Darth Sidious said softly. "Yes, he will take care of you."

CHAPTER 16

Bail Organa's coordinates were closer than Obi-Wan had expected. It didn't take long for him to reach the Alderaan starcruiser. The first thing he saw when he entered the ship was Master Yoda, standing placidly next to the worried-looking Senator.

"You made it!" Senator Organa said.

"Master Kenobi, dark times are these." Yoda's gravelly voice sounded refreshingly ordinary after everything that had happened. "Good to see you, it is."

"You were attacked by your clones, also?" Obi-Wan asked.

Yoda nodded. "With the help of the Wookiees, barely escape, I did."

If Master Yoda says he barely escaped, it must have been a hair-raising trip! It's a pily he'll never say anything more about it. "How many other Jedi managed to survive?"

Yoda bowed his head. "We've heard from . . . none."

None? Obi-Wan stared, speechless.

Bail Organa nodded in confirmation. "I saw thousands of troops attack the Jedi Temple. That's why I went looking for Yoda."

"Have you had any contact with the Temple?" Surely *someone* must be left. Master Windu . . . Kit Fisto . . . Anakin! Anakin was on Coruscant — had he been at the Temple?

"Received the coded retreat signal, we have," Yoda said.

The one that requests all Jedi to return to Coruscant! But if the clones were in control of the Temple . . .

"The war is over," Bail Organa said, his voice was bitter.

One of the pilots appeared in the doorway. "We are receiving a message from the Chancellor's office."

"Send it through," Bail told him.

A moment later, the oily voice of Mas Amedda, Chancellor Palpatine's chief aide, filled the room. "Senator Organa, the Supreme Chancellor of the Republic requests your presence at a special session of the Senate."

"Tell the Chancellor I will be there," Bail said.

"Very well," Mas Amedda replied, and the transmission ended.

Bail looked at Yoda and Obi-Wan. "Do you think it's a trap?"

"I don't think so," Obi-Wan replied after a moment's consideration. "The Chancellor won't be able to control thousands of star systems without keeping the Senate intact." Bail looked with concern at the two Jedi, and Obi-Wan replied to his unasked question about returning to the Jedi Temple. "We *have* to go back. If there are other stragglers, they will fall into the trap and be killed."

Yoda looked at him and nodded. He didn't have to say anything. They would go to the Jedi Temple and destroy the signal beacon that was calling other Jedi home to die. And perhaps — just perhaps — they would also learn how all of this had happened.

Bail parted from Obi-Wan and Yoda at the Senate landing platform. The two Jedi used their mind-clouding abilities to pass the red guards, then raised their hoods and slipped off. Bail watched them go with considerable misgiving. They were undoubtedly two of the best and most powerful Jedi in the galaxy, and they were warned and ready — but there were thousands of clone troops and security guards. If they were discovered, and it came to a battle . . .

But there was nothing he could do about that. He told Captain Antilles to keep the starcruiser ready to leave at any moment. Then, signaling his aides, he started for the Senate.

It was a shock to see the Senate building looking so . . . normal. The endless lines of traffic flowed around it at all levels, as if nothing unusual were happening. It was even more of a shock to see the sinister, hooded figure in the central pod, flanked by Mas Amedda and Sly Moore. The voice *sounded* like Chancellor Palpatine, but —

Then Bail heard the words the Chancellor was speaking: "The attempt on my life has left me scarred and deformed, but I assure you, my resolve has never been stronger."

Well, that explains the hood. Bail missed the next few sentences as he looked for the Naboo pod. Senator Padmé Amidala would tell him what he'd missed. He hurried over. "I was held up," he said in a low voice. "What happened?"

Padmé looked at him with shadowed eyes. "The Chancellor has been elaborating on a plot by the Jedi to overthrow the Senate."

"That's not true!"

But Padmé only looked at him hopelessly and said, "He's been presenting evidence all afternoon."

And the Senate will go along with it, just as they always do. But why would the Chancellor want to destroy the Jedi? With the war over —

As if he could hear what Bail was thinking, the

voice from the central podium announced, "The war is over! The Separatists have been defeated, and the Jedi rebellion has been foiled. We stand on the threshold of a new beginning."

The Senate burst into applause. As the noise went on and on, Bail stared at the hooded figure of the Chancellor in bewilderment. Now was the time for the Chancellor to give up his emergency powers, to return the Republic to its full democratic status. But the Jedi . . .

The applause began to die. The Chancellor held up his hand for quiet. When the arena was silent at last, he said, "In order to ensure our security and continuing stability, the Republic will now be reorganized into the First Galactic Empire, which I assure you will last for ten thousand years!"

Empire? Bail stared, stunned. He saw the same look on Padmé Amidala's face. Of all the possibilities, they had never anticipated anything like *this*! And the Senate was applauding! Palpatine went on, describing his new Empire in glowing terms, and with each sentence, the applause grew louder. Padmé looked away, and Bail saw tears in her eyes.

"So this is how liberty dies," she said softly. "With thunderous applause . . ."

Bail's mind began to move at last. He was a Senator; he could speak out against this . . . abomination. He started to stand, and Padmé put a restraining hand on his arm. He stared at her. "We cannot let this happen!" he said. Surely she agreed with him!

But Padmé shook her head. "Not now!" she said urgently. She glanced toward the podium, and then toward the entrances, and for the first time Bail noticed the red-clad guards and clone troopers standing at attention. They had always been there, it seemed; first, as part of the ceremony and respect due the Senate, and later, during the war, as a security measure to protect the Senators. But just who would they be protecting now?

Feeling cold, Bail relaxed back into his seat. Padmé nodded sadly. "There will be a time," she said, but she sounded as if it was more of a hope or a dream than a certainty.

Yes. There will be a time, Bail thought. He stared at the figure on the podium, and felt his face harden. He had been devoted to democracy all his life. He would spend the rest of it trying to restore what the Chancellor — no, Emperor, now — had taken away.

It hurt Obi-Wan to see black smoke billowing from the Jedi Temple. It hurt more to enter and find clones dressed in Jedi robes, waiting to ambush any real Jedi who came in. But what hurt the most was seeing the bodies of beings he had known and worked with, lying everywhere, and the Padawans and younglings. No one had survived.

Most disturbing of all were the bodies that had been killed, not by laser blasts, but by a lightsaber. *The Sith Lord!* Obi-Wan thought. Who else would use a lightsaber against Jedi? Obi-Wan swallowed hard. It had to be the Sith. Nobody else would . . . it *had to be him.*

Obi-Wan and Yoda had no trouble disposing of the first few clones they encountered. Once they were inside, they had even less trouble avoiding the others. The Jedi Temple was an enormous warren of passages and rooms; it took new Padawans years to learn their way around all of the sections. The clones had been there for less than a day.

Still, avoiding the clones took time. It was full night by the time they reached the main control center. Yoda stood guard while Obi-Wan reset the beacon and then added a few twists to hide what he had done. When Yoda gave him an impatient look, Obi-Wan explained, "I've recalibrated the code to warn any surviving Jedi away." That was much better than simply disabling the beacon.

"Good." Yoda nodded his approval. "To discover the recalibration, a long time it will take. To change it back, longer still." He gestured toward the door. "Hurry."

But Obi-Wan shook his head and crossed to the

hologram area. As he reached for the switch that would replay the recordings, Yoda said gently, "Master Obi-Wan, the truth you already know. To face it will only cause you anger and pain."

No. He had to watch the killings. He needed to see the face of the Sith Lord who had helped butcher all the Jedi in the Temple. "I must *know*, Master." His finger hit the button.

A hologram sprang up, showing the carnage in grim detail. Clone troopers fired on unsuspecting Jedi, cutting them down. And then a lightsaber flashed, held by a cloaked figure who cut down Jedi after Jedi, and Obi-Wan leaned forward. The figure turned. It was Anakin.

"It can't be," Obi-Wan whispered, heartbroken. "It can't be!"

But the holographic recording was pitiless. It played back the fight, exactly as it had occurred, and Obi-Wan had to watch Anakin kill and kill again. And then another figure entered the pickup, hidden beneath a hood. To Obi-Wan's horror, Anakin turned and knelt before it.

"The traitors have been destroyed, Lord Sidious," Anakin said.

"Good, good." The voice — that was Chancellor Palpatine! *He* was Darth Sidious, the Sith Lord? "You have done well, my new apprentice. Do you feel your power growing?"

"Yes, my Master," Anakin said, and Obi-Wan shuddered.

"Lord Vader, your skills are unmatched by any Sith before you," the cloaked figure said. "Now go, and bring peace to the Empire."

Empire?! Obi-Wan's fingers flew over the hologram keys, shutting off the scene that was far too painful to continue watching. Instead, he searched the holovid network for recent news. In seconds, the two Jedi learned what had been happening in the Senate while they had been slipping through the silent halls of the Jedi Temple. Chancellor Palpatine — the Sith Lord Darth Sidious — had declared an Empire instead of the Republic. The Sith ruled the galaxy once more.

Obi-Wan switched off the hologram completely, and the two Jedi stood in silence. How long had Darth Sidious been planning this? He had used the war, obviously — Count Dooku had been a Sith. Then Obi-Wan remembered: the first Sith he had encountered, back when he was still a Padawan. The Sith with the double-sided lightsaber, who had killed his Master, Qui-Gon Jinn. Did this plot go back that far?

Yes, it had to. He saw it, now, the whole clever, subtle plan. The Jedi knew that Darth Sidious had urged the Trade Federation to start the long-ago war on Naboo. Now Obi-Wan could see the true purpose of that war: to provide the opportunity for Senator Palpatine to become Supreme Chancellor

Palpatine. And then Palpatine must have seduced Count Dooku to the dark side, so that by the time his term as Chancellor was running out, the Separatists would be ready to start a larger war. Because of the Separatist threat, the Senate had begged Palpatine to stay on as Chancellor, and granted him more and more "emergency powers" in an effort to win a war that always *seemed* about to finish, but never was quite won.

Even the clone troops — the Jedi had accepted without question that Master Sifo-Dyas had arranged for their creation. But Sifo-Dyas was long dead. And that bounty hunter, the one who had provided the original genetic material for the clones . . . he'd told Obi-Wan that a man named Tyranus had recruited him. Obi-Wan had thought it was another lie; they'd found no man named Tyranus. *But I'll bet there was a Darth Tyranus! Why didn't I see it then?*

The war had thinned the ranks of the Jedi, and spread those who remained out over many worlds, so they would be easy prey when the time came for the final attack. And now — now only the two of them were left here. Obi-Wan could still hope that others had survived elsewhere, but the devastation he had seen in the last few hours had convinced him that no other Jedi remained alive on Coruscant.

Yoda broke the silence at last, saying what they both knew. "Destroy the Sith, we must."

Not just Emperor Palpatine; the Sith. There are

always two, a Master and an apprentice. *Two of them, and two of us. And one of them is —* "Send me to kill the Emperor," Obi-Wan said. He bowed his head. "I will not kill Anakin."

Yoda gave him a stern look. "To destroy this Lord Sidious, strong enough, you are not."

I know, but — "Anakin's like my brother," Obi-Wan said in anguish. "I cannot do this."

"Twisted by the dark side, young Skywalker has become," Yoda said firmly. "The boy you trained, gone is. Consumed by Darth Vader."

Obi-Wan flinched. "How could it have come to this?"

"To question, no time there is." Yoda started toward the door of the control room.

"I don't know where the Emperor sent him," Obi-Wan said, in a last, desperate attempt to avoid the duty he knew he must face. "I have no idea where to look."

"Use your feelings, Obi-Wan, and find him, you will," Yoda said, as if he were instructing a reluctant Padawan. "Visit the new Emperor, my task is." He looked at Obi-Wan with sympathy and understanding, but no pity. "May the Force be with you."

"May the Force be with you, Master Yoda," Obi-Wan replied. Yoda was right, as usual. He *did* know where to start looking for Anakin.

CHAPTER 17

Padmé was still awake when the alarm went off. She reached for the laser pistol she kept hidden by her bed, but the noise stopped almost at once. A false signal? She checked the readouts and saw that C-3PO had shut off the alarm. Swiftly, she pulled on a robe and went downstairs. C-3PO wouldn't deliberately let in an enemy, but he didn't always have the best judgment. And these days, it wasn't always clear who was an enemy, and who wasn't.

She heard voices as she came down the stairs. C-3PO was talking to — "Master Kenobi!" Padmé hurried down the last few steps as the protocol droid discreetly withdrew. "Oh, Obi-Wan, thank goodness you're alive!"

"The Republic has fallen, Padmé," Obi-Wan said gravely. "The Jedi Order is no more."

"I know." Padmé gazed at him, seeing the new lines in his face. "It's hard to believe." She took a deep breath. "But the Senate is still intact. There is some hope."

"No, Padmé," Obi-Wan said sadly. "It's over. The Sith now rule the galaxy, as they did before the Republic."

Padmé stared. "The *Sith*?" It was Palpatine who was in charge of the Repub — of the Empire. Surely Obi-Wan didn't mean that *Palpatine* was a Sith Lord!

"I'm looking for Anakin," Obi-Wan went on. "When was the last time you saw him?"

"Yesterday," Padmé said cautiously. Her head was spinning. Anakin had told her that his loyalties lay with the Republic, and with the Chancellor . . . but if the Chancellor was a Sith and the Republic no longer existed, what did that mean? And if there really *had* been a Jedi plot — no, no, she couldn't believe that, but still . . . she couldn't tell Obi-Wan too much until she understood.

"Do you know where he is now?"

She couldn't look at Obi-Wan's tired, worried face and lie to him. Her eyes fell. "No."

"Padmé, I need your help," Obi-Wan said. "He's in grave danger."

"From the Sith?" Padmé felt a moment's relief. Anakin was a Jedi; if the Sith were, somehow, behind everything that had happened, it made sense that he was in danger. But Obi-Wan was shaking his head, and her heart went cold even before she heard his words.

"Anakin has turned to the dark side."

"You're wrong!" Padmé cried. "How can you say that?"

"I've seen a security hologram of him killing . . . younglings."

"Not Anakin!" Padmé protested. "He couldn't!" But he had, once before — when he murdered the Sand People who'd killed his mother. *He was angry then. He lost control. He wouldn't just . . . He* wouldn't!

Obi-Wan was still talking, saying more horrible things — that Palpatine was a Sith Lord and Anakin his new apprentice. "I don't believe you!" Padmé burst out. "I can't."

The tired, sad voice stopped. "I must find him," Obi-Wan said after a moment.

But if he's — if you think he's a Sith . . . "You're going to kill him, aren't you?" she said, half accusing, half begging him to deny it.

Obi-Wan did not deny it. His head bent, and he said softly, "He has become a very great threat."

Overcome with horror, Padmé sank onto the nearest chair. She saw Obi-Wan's face change, and realized that she had let her robe twist close around her, so that he could see the unmistakable outline of her pregnancy. Too late, she pulled the robe away. "I can't —"

"Anakin's the father, isn't he?" Obi-Wan said gently. When she did not answer, he shook his head. "I'm so sorry." He pulled up his hood and walked toward the veranda. Padmé saw an airspeeder there; that must have been what set off the alarm. She felt torn. If Obi-Wan was right, she should call him back and tell him where Anakin had gone. But she *couldn't* betray Anakin. But —

The airspeeder took off. Obi-Wan was gone. Padmé's head bowed, and she found herself staring at the japor necklace. *Anakin.* She needed him here, now, to explain away all this horror. But Anakin was on Mustafar.

A long time later, Padmé looked up. With decision, she crossed to a comlink. "Captain Typho, prepare an interstellar skiff," she said, then turned back to her bedroom to dress. If Anakin was on Mustafar, she would go to him.

Obi-Wan slipped through the darkness at the edge of the landing platform. Trailing Padmé hadn't been difficult. Though she had been in danger many times, she had never learned to watch the shadows around her for possible threats, and her security guards had no reason to suspect that she might be followed. *She always believes the best of everyone, until she's forced to see the worst*, he thought sadly. Such faith should be a strength, not a weakness.

Judging from Captain Typho's tone, her security officer was very unhappy with the Senator at the moment. "My lady," the captain was saying, "let me come with you."

"There is no danger," Padmé told him. "The fighting is over, and . . . this is personal."

They've probably been arguing ever since they left the Senator's apartment, Obi-Wan thought.

Captain Typho paused at the foot of the landing ramp and bowed. "As you wish, my lady," he said formally. "But I strongly disagree."

"I'll be all right, Captain," Padmé said softly. "This is something I must do myself." She waited until the captain returned to the speeder and took off. Then she and her protocol droid climbed the ramp into the skiff. The skiff's engines started and the ramp began to retract.

Now! Obi-Wan thought, and leaped. He landed lightly on the end of the ramp and dove into the skiff just before the outside door closed. Padmé and her droid were in the cockpit. They didn't see him enter, and by the time the ship was safely in space, Obi-Wan had found a place to hide. All he had to do now was wait.

Outside the underground door of the office at the base of the Senate, Yoda paused. This was the domain of Mas Amedda, once the Vice-Chair of the Senate and now Chancellor — *Emperor* Palpatine's majordomo. Here, Mas Amedda prepared to run the Senate meetings; it was from this chamber that the Chancellor's podium rose into the center of the Senate. And tonight, the Force told him, it was here that Palpatine had come to see the finish of his evil plan.

Softly, Yoda approached the chamber. All four of the beings in the room — the two red guards, Mas Amedda, and the hooded figure of Darth Sidious — were too focused on the hologram in the center of the room to notice him. Darth Vader, who had been the Jedi Anakin Skywalker, had apparently been reporting.

"— taken care of, my Master," Vader said.

"Good, good," Sidious said. "Send a message to all ships of the Trade Federation. Tell them the Separatist leaders have been wiped out.

"Very good, my lord."

"You have done well, Lord Vader."

"Thank you, my Master."

As the hologram faded, Yoda stumped into the room. Before the guards could react, he used the Force to fling them against the walls. They collapsed in motionless heaps as Yoda said to the Sith Lord, "A new apprentice, you have, Chancellor. Or should I call you 'Emperor'?"

"Master Yoda." The Emperor inclined his head. "You survived."

"Surprised?"

"Your arrogance blinds you, Master Yoda," Darth Sidious hissed. "Now you will experience the full power of the dark side." He raised his arms, and the Force pulsed as blue lightning blasted Yoda across the room.

Mas Amedda looked from the Chancellor to Yoda, his eyes narrowed maliciously. He turned and left the room. Another wave of dark power lifted Yoda and flung him hard against the wall. Yoda used the Force to cushion the impact, but he pretended to be knocked unconscious. *A surprise, I will give him.*

"I have waited a long time for this moment, my little green friend," Darth Sidious sneered. He stepped forward, and Yoda pushed off, propelling himself straight at the Sith Lord. He knocked Darth Sidious over the desk and stared down at him.

"At an end your rule is," Yoda told the Emperor. "And not short enough it was, I must say." He ignited his lightsaber and brought it down, to be met by the Emperor's blood-red Sith blade.

CHAPTER 18

Even from space, Mustafar glowed like a hot ember; as her ship neared the surface, Padmé saw rivers of lava and oceans of molten rock. Fissures leaked fire from the heart of the planet, and smoke rose from cracks and vents on the blackened surface. It was hard to control the skiff in the shifting air currents, but eventually C-3PO fought it to a safe landing.

Through the cockpit window, she saw Anakin running eagerly toward the landing platform. Hastily, she unstrapped and ran out to meet him. His embrace reassured her; his arms made her feel secure once more. "It's all right," he murmured. "You're safe now." She looked up gratefully, and he said, "What are you doing out here?"

All the things she had been pushing out of her mind since leaving Coruscant came flooding back, and she looked down. "Obi-Wan told me terrible things."

She felt Anakin stiffen. "What things?"

"He said you have turned to the dark side," Padmé blurted. "That you killed younglings." Her voice sounded accusing, even to her own ears. This wasn't the way she'd meant to ask him for the truth.

"Obi-Wan is trying to turn you against me," Anakin said, and she heard the stirring of a terrible anger in his voice.

"He cares about us," Padmé told him. "He wants to help you."

"Don't lie to me, Padmé," Anakin said. His arms dropped. "I have become more powerful than any Jedi dreamed of. And I've done it for you. To protect *you*."

What has that to do with Obi-Wan? With what he said? But she knew. It was Anakin's excuse for whatever fearful things he had done. As if saying "I did it for love; I did it for you" would make it right. Padmé drew back. "I don't want your *power*." She swallowed. "I don't want your protection." She reached for him, pleading, wanting him to be the man she loved. "Anakin, all I want is your love."

"Love won't save you," Anakin said, and it sounded like a threat. "Only my new powers can do that."

"At what cost?" Padmé asked. "You are a good person. Don't do this."

"I won't lose you the way I lost my mother!"

"Come away with me." She put a hand on her swelling stomach. "Help me raise our child. Leave everything else behind while we still can."

"Don't you see?" Anakin leaned forward eagerly. "We don't have to run away anymore. I have brought peace to the Republic. I am more powerful than the Chancellor. I can overthrow him, and together you and I can rule the galaxy. We can make things the way we want them to be."

Padmé recoiled. "I don't believe what I'm hearing! Obi-Wan was right. You've changed."

"I don't want to hear any more about Obi-Wan!" Anakin's temper burst loose. Her fear must have shown on her face, because he made a visible effort to control himself. "The Jedi turned against me," he said more softly. "The Republic turned against me. Don't you turn against me, too."

I'm not against you. I'm against what you've done, and what you're planning to do. "I don't know you anymore," she told him. Couldn't he see what he was doing? Couldn't he feel her heart breaking? "I'll never stop loving you, but you are going down a path I cannot follow." In despair, she reached for the connection they had had through the Force, for that one moment when she had known him completely even though they hadn't been together.

But even a Jedi couldn't create a Force connection just by trying, and Padmé was no Jedi. Desperate as she was, she could find only a faint thread of what they had shared, thinner than a strand of spider silk. It still joined her with a familiar trace of . . . goodness? Sensing that, she felt a stirring of hope. She spoke to that part of him, trying to call back the Anakin who was her husband, her lover, the father of their child. "Stop now," she begged. "Come back! I love you."

For a moment — for the barest instant — she thought she would succeed. Then Anakin's expression changed. "Liar!" he cried.

He was staring at something behind her. Padmé turned, and saw Obi-Wan standing in the door of the skiff. *He tricked me!* "No!" she said, knowing that this new Anakin would never listen to her now.

"You've betrayed me!" Rage made Anakin's face unrecognizable. He lifted his hand and curled his fingers into a fist. Padmé felt herself choking, unable to breathe.

Don't! Don't kill our child! But she had no breath to cry out with, and even the ghost of the Force connection was gone. The world darkened, and she felt herself falling. Her last conscious thought was a feeling of relief. She would rather die here, now, than live and have to watch what her Anakin had become.

Obi-Wan ran forward as Padmé collapsed. He flung his cloak aside, and bent to check on her. She was still alive, and not, he sensed, in immediate danger. But Anakin was already there, his face an angry mask. "You turned her against me!" he cried, flinging the accusation against Obi-Wan.

"You have done that yourself," Obi-Wan told him. Here, in Anakin's presence, he could feel what the hologram couldn't show him: the roiling cloud of the dark side that surrounded his former apprentice. It made the coming duty a little — a very little — easier. "You've let the dark side twist your point of view until now . . . now you are the very thing you swore to destroy."

"Don't muke me kill you," Anakin said.

The words struck straight to Obi-Wan's heart. Surely something of his friend and student was still left, for him to say that? But even if there was, no Jedi had ever returned from the dark side. Yoda had warned them all, over and over, throughout their training: *If once you start down the dark path, forever will it dominate your destiny.* Anakin had turned to the dark side. It was too late for him. Sadly, Obi-Wan said, "My allegiance is to the Republic, Anakin. To democracy."

"You are with me, or you are against me," Anakin replied.

"Only a Sith Lord deals in absolutes, Anakin," Obi-Wan told him, and ignited his lightsaber. *Now I will do what I must.*

Anakin's face twisted as he ignited his own weapon, and the battle began.

Strong, this Sith Lord is, Yoda thought as their lightsabers whirled and clashed and whirled again.

It should not have been a surprise. With the strength of the dark side growing, the Sith must, logically, have grown stronger, too. But always before, his own years of study and practice and his own strength with the Force had been more than enough to prevail. This time, he wasn't sure.

But Palpatine didn't seem entirely sure, either. Suddenly, he launched himself into the air, heading for the door. Yoda did a back flip, bounced off the wall, and reached the entrance before him. "If so powerful you are, why leave?"

"You will not stop me," the new Emperor croaked. "Darth Vader will become more powerful than either of us."

"Faith in your new apprentice, misplaced may be," Yoda replied. *As is your faith in the dark side of the Force.* Even if Palpatine killed him here, today, the dark side would not truly win. For the dark side was anger, hatred, despair — all the forces of ruin and decay. Powerful, they were, to tear down and destroy, but they could not build anything lasting. Palpatine's ten-thousand-year Galactic Empire would be lucky to outlast his lifetime.

That thought gave Yoda new energy, and he pressed his attack. He drove Palpatine back across the room, into the Chancellor's podium. Palpatine hit the controls, and the podium began to rise, carrying him up into the Senate. But the podium moved slowly; Yoda had plenty of time to flip himself into the air and land beside the Emperor, to continue the fight.

As the podium rose into the Senate arena, the fight intensified. Twice, Yoda came near to pushing Palpatine over the edge. They were high enough now that a fall could be fatal, even to a Sith Lord. *Or a Jedi Master.* The cramped space within the pod left little room for maneuvering.

An end, I must make. Yoda redoubled the speed of his blows. Palpatine parried one, then another — and then the red lightsaber spun out of his hands and over the edge. Yoda raised his weapon for the final blow.

Force lightning spat from the Emperor's gray fingers, surrounding Yoda in a blue nimbus. But Yoda had faced Force lightning before. To deflect the first bolts, he had to stop his intended strike at the Emperor. Once his initial surprise was over, he reached out to the living Force. The lightning bent, arcing back toward the Emperor.

"Destroy you, I will," Yoda said grimly. "Just as Master Kenobi, your apprentice will destroy."

The Sith Lord only redoubled his attack. Hurling Force lightning, the Emperor backed away, to the very edge of the platform. Following him was like walking against hurricane winds. Never had Yoda faced one so strong in the dark side. Before he came within reach, a particularly strong blast knocked Yoda out of the pod.

As he plunged over the edge, Yoda realized that Palpatine was right about one thing. He, Yoda, had indeed been arrogant. *It is a flaw more and more common among Jedi*, he had told Obi-Wan once. *Too sure of themselves, they are.* And he had fallen into the same trap himself.

He landed much sooner than he had expected, in an empty Senate pod floating below the Chancellor's. As he climbed to his feet, the pod jerked, throwing him sideways and knocking him down once more. Palpatine was using the dark side to rip more pods free, crashing them into Yoda's pod to keep him off-balance.

This game, two can play. Yoda reached out with the Force and caught one of the hurtling pods. He threw it back at Palpatine, who barely dodged in time. Then Yoda leaped, using the flying pods to get back up to the Chancellor's level.

As he reached Palpatine's pod, the Sith Lord hit him with another blast of blue lightning that knocked Yoda's lightsaber out of his hand. Palpatine's lips curled in anticipated triumph, and the dark side pulsed as he drew even more Force lightning to his bidding.

Yoda caught it. The blue energy built into a glowing ball in his hand, ready to throw back at the Sith

Lord the moment his attack stopped. But Palpatine didn't stop; the Force lightning came in a steady crackle, building more and more, until neither of them could hold it any longer, and the blast knocked them both out of the pod.

Palpatine was larger and heavier; he managed to catch hold of the edge of the pod as he fell. But Yoda was small and light. The explosion threw him high into the air, with nothing to grab to break his fall. Half-stunned, he began the long fall to the Senate floor.

CHAPTER 19

As Anakin's lightsaber hummed toward him, a calm certainty filled Obi-Wan. Anakin was going to kill him. Oh, he'd make Anakin work for it. He'd fight with everything he had. But he was positive, with the sureness that came from any Force-driven insight, that he would die at Anakin's hands.

His lightsaber came up in an instinctive parry. They had sparred together so often that they knew each other's favorite moves. Obi-Wan hardly had to think to counter Anakin's attack. Lightsabers humming, they battled their way down the hall and into the control center. It felt . . . familiar, like another practice session, except for the exploding equipment.

He saw the same emotions reflected on Anakin's face. "Don't make me destroy you," his former apprentice said again. Then his expression changed to a sneer. "You're no match for the dark side."

"I've heard that before, Anakin," Obi-Wan said. "But I never thought I'd hear it from you."

They were in the conference room now. There were headless and limbless bodies on the floor; Obi-Wan recognized several of the Separatist leaders. *Anakin has been here before,* he thought. But still his arms moved, weaving light into a deadly shield against all of Anakin's blows.

Anakin did a back flip onto the table to gain the high ground. But Obi-Wan had been expecting something like that, and did not follow. Instead, he threw himself into a long slide, bowling Anakin over.

As he fell, Anakin lost his grip on his lightsaber. Obi-Wan caught it and stared at it in surprise. *How can Anakin kill me, if he doesn't have a lightsaber?* Then Anakin charged him. Before Obi-Wan could swing his own weapon, Anakin was on him. His left hand gripped Obi-Wan's right wrist, holding off the deadly lightsaber; the mechanical right hand fought to repossess his own weapon.

Durasteel and servomotors proved stronger than flesh and bone. Anakin wrenched his lightsaber away, and attacked once more.

Out into the hall, they fought, then onto a balcony above a river of lava. A slender pipe led from the control center to a collection plant on the far side of the river. As Anakin's attack intensified, Obi-Wan was forced onto the pipe, where a single misstep would send him plunging into the fire.

*   *   *

As Yoda fell, he reached out to slow his fall with all the mastery of the Force he had learned in his long years. It was enough, barely. He landed hard, but not too hard.

Bruised and battered, but alive, he crawled into a service chute. There would be no second chance to kill the Emperor; he would summon his clone troops immediately for protection. All Yoda could do now was escape.

Activating his comlink, he called to the one person on Coruscant he knew he could still trust — Bail Organa. The Senator did not waste time demanding explanations, and he followed Yoda's instructions as carefully as any Jedi would have. Sooner than he would have believed, Yoda dropped from an access hatch into Bail's speeder and was carried away into the night.

Away from the Senate, Bail gave Yoda a questioning look. Yoda told him the only thing that mattered. "Failed, I have."

Bail nodded somberly, and turned his speeder toward the spaceport. *Obi-Wan, we will look for*, Yoda thought. *Better fortune, he may have had.*

From the damaged podium, Darth Sidious watched his clone troopers search the shadows. Mas Amedda had brought them, too late to help do anything but clean up.

Sidious knew he should have been pleased with the outcome of the fight. He had won, though it had been a near thing. But an uneasiness was growing within him, a sense of some threat not yet resolved.

Below, the clone commander boarded a Senate pod and rose to the level of the podium. "There is no sign of his body, sir," he reported, saluting.

"Then he is not dead," Mas Amedda replied.

Sidious nodded and reached out with the dark side, trying to sense where his enemy was hiding. As he did, the feeling of risk grew stronger, and he understood. Not a threat to him, but to his apprentice. He must see to this personally. "Double your search," he told the clone commander, though he doubted they would find anything. He turned to Mas Amedda. "Tell Captain Kagi to prepare my shuttle for immediate takeoff. I sense Lord Vader is in danger."

Mas Amedda bowed. "Yes, my Master."

Crossing the collection pipe was difficult, even for a Jedi. At one point, Obi-Wan slipped and nearly fell into the lava, but his Jedi reflexes and agility let him recover. On the far side, Anakin rushed him again, driving him back onto the collection plates.

But the collection plant had never been designed to take the weight of two men, and in the heat of the battle in the control room, they had smashed the shield controls that protected the plant from fiery lava, weakening the structure. A spray of lava from the river that melted one of the supports provided the final straw. A huge section of a collection arm broke away and fell into the lava, carrying the two Jedi with it.

Still the fight continued, even as the collection tower sank slowly into the lava. And still, neither man could gain an advantage.

But that's not really true, Obi-Wan thought as he ducked and wove and parried. Both he and Anakin felt the anguish of their need to kill the other. But Anakin had turned to the dark side, and despair and pain strengthened the dark side. It gave him an advantage Obi-Wan could not match. Unless he let go of his own despair and let the living Force move him — the Force that bound all living things together, even Obi-Wan and this new, deadly, evil Anakin.

It was hard. It was, perhaps, the hardest thing he had ever tried to do. For in letting go of his anguish, his despair, and his pain, he would have to let go of the Anakin who was his student, his brother, and his dearest friend. He'd have to admit that this time, he could not save the man who had saved his life so many times, whose life he had saved at least as often.

Obi-Wan couldn't do it. As the collection tower sank farther into the lava, he looked for a way to escape. A droid platform floated on air near the tower. Obi-Wan took another swipe at Anakin, then grabbed a hanging cable and swung out toward the platform. At the height of his swing, he flipped himself into the air, landing precisely.

The platform wobbled, but it held his weight. He leaned to one side, steering it away from the collection tower. Perhaps the sinking tower and the lava would do what he had been unable to finish.

But when he looked back, Anakin was standing on a worker droid, coming up fast. "Your combat skills have always been poor," he taunted. "You're called the Negotiator because you can't fight!"

"I have failed you, Anakin," Obi-Wan told him. "I was never able to teach you to think."

Anakin nodded. "I should have known the Jedi were plotting to take over."

"From the Sith!" Obi-Wan cried, shocked. "Anakin, Chancellor Palpatine is evil."

"From the Jedi point of view!" Anakin retorted. "From my point of view, the Jedi are evil."

The words stabbed at Obi-Wan, even though he knew that Anakin was speaking out of his own pain. He felt the dark side grow stronger, feeding on his despair. And then, as Anakin came close enough to swing his lightsaber once more, the Jedi in Obi-Wan rose up and at last he did the thing he hadn't thought he could do.

He let go. Calm, centered, free — for the

moment — of sorrow and despair, resting in the living Force as he had been trained to do, Obi-Wan Kenobi looked at his former friend and student, and did the unexpected. He made a soaring leap into the air and landed on the high bank of the lava river.

"It's over, Anakin," he said, looking down. "I have the high ground. Don't try it."

"You underestimate the power of the dark side!" Anakin shot back, and with the last word, he jumped.

And Obi-Wan's lightsaber moved, slicing through Anakin's knees and then coming up to take his remaining hand. Anakin's lightsaber fell at Obi-Wan's feet. What was left of Anakin fell on the burning black sand almost at the edge of the lava.

Anakin — no, Obi-Wan reminded himself, not Anakin. Darth Vader. Darth Vader scrabbled at the sand with his metal arm, trying to pull himself away from the lava river. Obi-Wan looked down at the maimed body, and at last felt tears sting his eyes. "You were the Chosen One," he said, not to Darth Vader, but to his dead friend Anakin, the man whose spirit Darth Vader had murdered. "You were supposed to destroy the Sith, not join them. You were to bring balance to the Force, not leave it in darkness." He swallowed hard. He couldn't see the body through his tears; he could barely make out the shine of Anakin's lightsaber on the ground at his feet.

"I hate you!" Vader screamed.

As Obi-Wan bent and picked up Anakin's fallen lightsaber, Darth Vader slipped too close to the lava, and his clothes caught fire. In an instant, the flames engulfed him, and he screamed. Obi-Wan stared in horror, unable to make himself move. But as the flames began to die, he murmured his response to Darth Vader's final cry of anger and hate: "You were my brother, Anakin. I loved you."

The screams died, and the flames. Dashing tears from his eyes, Obi-Wan turned away — and saw a shuttle coming in to land. Whoever it was, Obi-Wan didn't want to meet him. He ran back to Padmé's skiff. C-3PO and R2-D2 had already taken Padmé on board, and he was glad. All he wanted now was to get away from this place. Later . . . later he might be able to think about what would come next.

CHAPTER 20

As the Imperial shuttle closed its wings and settled on the topmost landing platform, Darth Sidious saw a small starship fleeing from Mustafar. But he could not order the shuttle into pursuit — the uneasy urgency was stronger than ever, and it was tied to the planet, not the ship.

The clone troopers disembarked first, fanning out through the quiet building to make sure nothing would endanger their Emperor. They found only bodies. Then, as Darth Sidious inspected the control room, one of the troopers came in through an exterior door.

"There's something out here," he reported.

That's it. As quickly as he could, Darth Sidious followed the troopers outside, onto the black sand banks of a lava river. A charred heap lay on one side. *No; it can't be!*

But it was. His promising new apprentice, who was to be the greatest Sith who'd ever lived — maimed and burned, perhaps dead. Darth Sidious ground his teeth in frustrated anger. Part of him wanted to turn on his heel and leave what was left of Darth Vader to burn to ashes in the rising lava. Even if he was alive, even if he could be saved, Vader would be crippled.

And not just with his mechanical limbs. The Force — dark side as well as light — was generated by living beings, and it took living flesh to manipulate it. Darth Vader would never be able to cast blue Force lightning; that required living hands, not metal ones. And with so much of his body replaced by machinery, he would never come close to the potential he'd had.

It was a great pity, Darth Sidious thought, controlling his anger, but perhaps not irreparable. Even diminished, Darth Vader would still be very strong, and there were no Jedi left to challenge him. Darth Sidious had seen to that himself. So he kept walking until he could bend over the body. And to his surprise, his apprentice *was* still alive.

Relief swept his doubts away. "Get a medical capsule immediately," Darth Sidious commanded, and clones ran off to do his bidding. Leaning down, he placed a hand on Darth Vader's forehead, using the dark side to keep him alive.

When they fled from Coruscant, Yoda left their destination to Bail Organa. The Senator chose an obscure archaeological project on the asteroid Polis Massa. There they set up a homing beacon, and waited hopefully for Obi-Wan.

With nothing to do but wait, Yoda automatically found a quiet room and sat down to meditate. The being who had been trying to contact him surely could not reach through the newly strengthened fog of the dark side, but the habit had become strong. And to his surprise, this time the contact succeeded.

Qui-Gon Jinn! No wonder the presence had felt familiar. *Still much to learn, there is.*

Patience, Qui-Gon responded. *You will have the time I did not. With my help, you will be able to merge with the Force at will, and still retain your individual consciousness.*

Eternal life, Yoda marveled.

The story of Darth Plagueis was true, in a way. The ability to defy death can be achieved, but only for oneself. It was never accomplished by Darth Plagueis, only by a Shaman of the Whills, and it will never be achieved by a Sith Lord. It is a state acquired through compassion, not greed.

To become one with the Force, and influence still have. The thought was stunning. *A power greater than all, it is.* Yoda bowed his head. *A great Jedi Master, you have become, Qui-Gon Jinn. Your apprentice, I gratefully become.*

He felt the former Jedi's approval, just before Bail

Organa entered to tell him that Obi-Wan was landing. The contact was broken, but Yoda knew that Qui-Gon would have no future difficulty in reaching him, now that he had done it once. At least some good news, there was to tell Obi-Wan.

When the skiff landed, Obi-Wan jumped from the pilot's chair and gently lifted the still-unconscious Padmé. Yoda and Bail were waiting at the bottom of the ramp. Bail took one shocked look at Padmé and said, "Take her to the medical center, quickly."

They have a medical center; good. Obi-Wan had been half afraid that the medical facilities on an isolated asteroid would be too primitive to deal with whatever ailed Padmé. She *should* have come around once Darth Vader stopped choking her, but she hadn't — but Obi-Wan didn't know much about pregnant women. Maybe something else was wrong.

With relief, he handed Padmé over to the medical droids and went to sit in the observation room with Bail and Yoda. Moments later, one of the droids came up to the window. "Medically, she is completely healthy," the droid said. "For reasons we can't explain, we are losing her."

"She's *dying*?" Obi-Wan said, horrified. *No, no!* He couldn't take another loss like this.

But the medical droid bobbed its head. "We don't know why. She has lost the will to live."

I know why, Obi-Wan thought. *Anakin has broken her heart.*

"We need to operate quickly if we are to save the babies," the droid continued. "She's carrying twins."

"Save them, we must," Yoda commanded. "They are our last hope."

The medical droids went to work. They insisted that Obi-Wan join them, though he wasn't sure what he could do. But the droids felt that human contact would help, and — these were Anakin's children, and this was the last thing Obi-Wan could do for his dead friend. He stood by, holding Padmé's hand and feeling helpless.

As the droids delivered the first of the babies, Padmé stirred. She looked at Obi-Wan in puzzlement; then she saw the medical droids and seemed to realize what was happening. "Is it a girl?" she whispered.

"We don't know," Obi-Wan said, feeling harried. "In a minute."

"It's a boy," the medical droid said, holding him up. The baby was wrinkled and red-faced, his eyes squeezed tightly shut against the light, but Padmé smiled and reached for him. "Luke," she said, her fingers just brushing his forehead.

"And a girl," the second droid said. Unlike her

brother, this baby's eyes were wide, and she stared in Padmé's direction as if she wanted to see and memorize her face.

"Leia," Padmé said.

"You have twins, Padmé," Obi-Wan told her. "They need you. Hang on!"

Padmé's head rolled back and forth on the bed in a gesture of negation. "I can't," she whispered. Wincing, she reached for Obi-Wan's hand. She was holding something — a carved piece of wood on a long cord.

"Save your energy," Obi-Wan told her, but she held up the carving as if it were something precious.

"Obi-Wan," Padmé gasped. "There *is* good in him." She paused, panting. "I know there . . . is . . . still . . ." Her voice faded, and her hand dropped away. Obi-Wan felt the life leave her.

She believed in Anakin until the end, he thought, and bowed his head. He didn't know whether his tears were for Padmé or for his lost friend, or both.

The medical capsule kept Darth Vader alive during the trip to Coruscant. Medical droids from the Imperial Rehabilitation Center on Coruscant, the best in the galaxy, were ready and waiting, thanks to the Emperor's urgent message. They examined their patient at once. Much work was necessary, they reported. The amputations alone would have been a simple matter of replacement; it was the burns that made matters so difficult. Special connections would be required to overcome the scarring. Worse, Darth Vader's lungs had been seared by the fire. He would need a permanent ventilator system in order to breathe. And —

"Do it," the Emperor snapped.

The droids bobbed their consent and went to work. Darth Sidious paced. Even an Emperor, even the Dark Lord of the Sith, with all the resources and technology of the new Galactic Empire behind him, can do little to hurry the healing process.

Much later, a medical droid appeared. "My lord, the construction is finished," the droid informed him. "He lives."

"Good," Darth Sidious said with something very like relief. "*Good.*"

The droid brought him to the operating room. A black figure lay on the operating table. Black gloves and boots covered the new mechanical limbs; a mirror shiny black mask hid the scarred face. The table began to tilt, moving the figure to an upright position. There was the sound of breathing.

Yes, Darth Sidious thought. *He will terrify them. And even if he is not as powerful as I had once hoped, he will still be far more powerful than anyone else.*

"Lord Vader," Darth Sidious said. "You may rise."

A deep voice, distorted by the speakers inside the mask, responded. "Yes, my Master." The helmet turned, as if the burned and weakened eyes within were scanning the room, adjusting to the screens in the helmet that magnified and intensified everything so that they could pretend to see. "Where is Padmé? Is she all right?"

And now, the final touch, Darth Sidious thought. *The words that will bind him forever to the dark side. And they won't even be a lie, not really.* "I'm afraid she died," he said, putting a hint of gentle sorrow and reproach into his voice. "It seems that in your anger, you killed her."

Vader groaned in protest. And then he screamed. Leaning forward, he broke the straps that had held him to the table, and screamed again. Things imploded and flew around the room — spare parts, droids, anything that wasn't tied down — as Darth Vader gave expression to his pain and despair.

And while Darth Vader screamed, Darth Sidious smiled. His apprentice was his, now. Forever.

The conference room on Bail Organa's starcruiser looked exactly like every other conference room Obi-Wan had ever sat in. He didn't want to be there. He didn't feel up to making decisions about the future, and he certainly didn't want to think about the past. But he and Yoda and Bail were the only ones left to decide. So there he sat, trying to make his tired brain think about what to do with the body of his best friend's wife, and with the two infants who were, perhaps, the last hope of the galaxy.

"To Naboo, send her body," Yoda said. "Pregnant, she must still appear. Hidden, safe, the children must be kept."

"Someplace where the Sith will not sense their presence," Obi-Wan said.

"Split up, they should be."

Bail Organa raised his head. "My wife and I will take the girl. We've always talked of adopting a baby girl. She will be loved with us."

Hidden in plain sight, Obi-Wan thought, and nodded. "What about the boy?"

"To Tatooine. To his family, send him."

Remembering that harsh, dry planet, Obi-Wan winced. But there was nowhere else, and Tatooine was a world on the margins — the Hutt crime lords who ruled it had never been part of the Galactic Republic, and they would keep their distance from the Empire as well. "I will take the child there, and watch over him," Obi-Wan said. He looked at Yoda, wanting reassurance he knew Yoda could not give him. "Master Yoda, do you think Anakin's twins will be able to defeat Darth Sidious?"

"Strong the Force runs, in the Skywalker line,"

Yoda replied. "Only hope, we can." He looked at Bail. "Done then, it is. Until the time is right, disappear we will."

Bail nodded and left to give orders to his pilot. Obi-Wan rose to leave as well.

"Wait a moment, Master Kenobi," Yoda said.

Obi-Wan turned, thinking *What now?*

"In your solitude on Tatooine, training I have for you."

"Training?" He had never heard of any Jedi training for Masters.

Yoda smiled. "An old friend has learned the path to immortality — your old Master, Qui-Gon Jinn."

"Qui-Gon?" Obi-Wan stared. "But . . . how?"

"The secrets of the Ancient Order of the Whills, he studied," Master Yoda said. "How to commune with him, I will teach you."

"I will be able to talk with him?"

Yoda nodded, and some of the old, old grief that had lived with Obi-Wan since his Master's death lifted. "How to join the Force, he will train you. Your consciousness you will retain, when one with the Force. Even your physical self, perhaps."

How ironic that we should discover this power now, when the Jedi are no more, Obi-Wan thought. Then he looked at Yoda. The Jedi were not gone. Not yet. He heard the thin, high wail of an infant echoing down the hall, and almost smiled. There was still hope for the future.

EPILOGUE

Senator Padmé Amidala was given a state funeral. Huge crowds lined the streets to pay their respects to their former Queen as the flower-draped open coffin rolled past. She was wearing the carved japor snippet her beloved Anakin had given her so long ago, when he was nine and she fourteen and war was unthinkable, and the Sith Lords a bad dream.

Obi-Wan and Yoda watched the funeral from Bail Organa's starcruiser. It was as close as they dared come. The Emperor's attention would surely be fixed on the funeral, and they would not take the risk of being found.

Shortly after, the Emperor took his new apprentice off to a remote area of the galaxy where construction of a new superweapon was just beginning — a gigantic space station with the power to destroy whole planets with a single laser blast.

Once the funeral was over, Bail Organa set his

cruiser on a carefully planned course to Alderaan. Shortly after the ship left Naboo, it flung two small escape pods in opposite directions along the Outer Rim. One carried Jedi Master Yoda toward the uninviting and uninhabited swamp planet of Dagobah; the other carried Jedi Master Obi-Wan Kenobi and a wailing infant boy in the direction of Tatooine. The girl, as planned, went on to Alderaan, to be raised as a princess by Bail Organa and his wife, the queen of Alderaan. She was joined by the droids R2-D2 and C-3PO.

When he reached Tatooine, Obi-Wan sold the escape pod for spare parts. In the crime-ridden city of Mos Eisley, the pod would be untraceable within hours. With the credits from the sale, Obi-Wan bought an eopie riding beast for the trek out to the small moisture farm where Anakin's stepbrother, Owen Lars, still lived. Owen and his wife Beru agreed to raise their nephew. Obi-Wan told them only that the boy's parents were both dead; he did not give any details of how Anakin and Padmé had died.

As the twin suns began to set, Obi-Wan rode into the Tatooine desert. In his pack, he carried Anakin's lightsaber. He would keep it, through the long, lonely exile, as a memento and a reminder — until the future day when he could give it to Anakin's son, Luke Skywalker.

Your Power Builds...
With Every Brick!

7252

7259

7256